FORTUNES
NECK

Kevin McDermott

ThickWinter Press

ThickWinter Press

ISBN: 978-0-578-17686-4

For my wife

It used to be that a hanging was remembered for years. If a child fell into a pond and drowned, if a building burned down on its occupants, people living in the places where these things happened were still talking about them fifty years later. The duration of conscious memory is shortened now. Stories go underground, living there like an urge. And then at the first opportunity they bubble up.

Fortunes Neck

.....See,
now they vanish,
The faces and places, with the self
Which, as it would, loved them,
To become renewed, transfigured,
in another pattern.

T.S. Elliot, "Little Gidding"

Things go way back. Even in the most thickly settled place it's not hard to imagine meadows, forest, hard silence. People as babies and then old. Trees branching and withering, cut down to make fields and plant corn, and then the fields abandoned. Even after three hundred years the ground around Fortunes Neck showed marks of the 17th Century—surprising in such a watery place. The center of everything was still Bring Street, the first street to be built in Fortunes Neck. It was cut through to carry timber to the Mattabesic River from up on Waterhouse Hill. Tree by tree they cut it all down—all the wood up there. Picture it, those men in short pants using hand-axes. They had the time, of course—where were they going? In the old days there was no end to enterprise.

The Weir family owned Waterhouse Hill. It was they who had the rights to strip the hardwood from up there. With the money he made selling the timber John Weir purchased slaves to prize out the stumps; into the 20th Century an occasional walker up on Waterhouse Hill might look down in the mud beside the path and find an ankle cuff or something like that, a souvenir of Weir's industry and a proof of history.

Weir planted everything he could think of up on his hill. With corn he had a little luck, but in general the soil was too dead for anything worthwhile growing. Weir had an idea of irrigating it and built an early form of piston engine to fill a cistern at the top of the hill. The machine never really worked except in spring when the Mattabesic flowed with enough volume to power the thing; even then the machine frequently choked on silt. Today the place is still called Waterhouse Hill after that water engine, though if you asked a local they most likely couldn't tell you anything about that.

When John Weir was done his hill was left naked forever. By the time of the American Revolution there was no one who remembered when Waterhouse Hill was ever anything but barren. Cursed by baldness was believed to be the way God made it.

Treeless hills should make us leery.

In 1794 John Weir's great grandson Roger married Sarah Croft. When Sarah died she deeded Waterhouse Hill to the town of Fortunes Neck. Into the 1940s people were still speaking of the hill as "the commonage", liking the quaintness of using such a term; so there's nothing new about nostalgia. As early as Civil War days people were homesick for the pastoral. In 1864 the Fortunes Neck Merchants Association (whose motto was "Librus et lux") invented a spring-tradition of picnicking up on the Hill.

In the places we live status may derive from all kinds of things—money (mainly money), handsomeness, talent, character. The Weir family had ancestry, with roots in Fortunes Neck that were planted in the 17th Century. They could look back three hundred years to the pilgrim Waterhouse family. The Weirs were never rich but they were steadily employed;

there was always a lot to do. After the original John Weir, the one who cleared the forest on Waterhouse Hill, his son Roger Weir owned one of the last really big slave holdings in New England. John Weir's cousin, Jane Croft, was almost hung for a witch in Fairfield, Connecticut. A neighbor accused her of casting spells on a romantic rival; Jane admitted her guilt and she was set free. The Weirs sent soldiers to the Revolution and the Civil War, and two became judges. Among the best-remembered person in the family was Frank, who drove the Railway Express wagon between Fortunes Neck and Springfield. Frank was famous for the time an Indian stole his pants. It was 1891, the year after Sitting Bull was shot. All around the country there were rumors of Ghost Dancers, even in the East and even in Massachusetts. One morning at dawn Frank was just a few miles out of town when the Indian—or somebody dressed like one—stepped in front of the REA wagon holding a shotgun. He pointed it up at Frank and yelled, "Pants! Pants!" Frank worked out that, as he put it, "the fella wanted my drawers, and at gunpoint who was I to ask him what for?" So Frank pulled off his pants and handed them over. It was a chilly morning and Frank covered his naked legs with a spare tarpaulin. He rode the whole way into Springfield like that. Everyone told the story for a long time.

Frank's son Warren enlarged on his father's association with REA to build a small freight-forwarding business in Fortunes Neck. His place was just at the bottom of Bring Street where the street ran into the river. (This was before the Bring Street bridge was put up.) Warren died at the young age of 43, though he left his family in reasonable prosperity.

Which was fortunate. His older child Millicent was an invalid suffering degenerative arthritis that began in childhood. She had to have constant care. The other child, a son, had expensive ambitions to be a doctor. The boy had that focus from an early age. In later years no one could remember when he wasn't called Doc.

People in Fortunes Neck wanted to think well of the Weir family. Even in the years before the Second World War the town was losing its village status. Hartford and Springfield grew and Fortunes Neck began to feel "closer in", as people said. The Weirs alluded to something native, to a continuing sense of *we* in opposition to *other*. But we have to make our own histories. It is no good looking for our stories in someone else.

One may become an orphan at any age. In 1925, the year she met Doc Weir, Jeannine Brown and her brother Laurence were each other's only family (but for an aunt and uncle in Shrewsbury, whom they detested). Since the influenza epidemic of 1919 they had been motherless, and five summers later they lost their father as well.

The father, Dominic Brown, was only 47 when he disappeared at sea. Until that time the Browns were a prominent family in their portion of New England—prominent more for wealth than lineage, so in that sense they were a family the reverse of the Weirs. They were Scots Irish who came up to Vermont in the 1850s. The grandfather made his money in quarries. All over the northeastern United States there are buildings still standing that were built with granite and marble from the Brown family's quarries. By the First World War that business was almost all played out. It was literally underwater, since the deeper the quarries were cut the more impossible they became to drain. By the twenties several were notorious tips for corpses, unwanted babies and rubbish generally. (One near Dartmouth was nicknamed "Lake Lacuna".) But there was still plenty of family capital for Dominic to sustain himself. He was a yachtsman. In August, 1924, he and two companions sailed out of Portsmouth bound for Brittany. They left in the hope of getting across the North Atlantic ahead of the late-summer weather. On the fourth day out Dominic took the overnight helm while his crewmates went below decks to sleep. The seas got up. In the morning the others found the stern rail broken and Dominic just gone.

The friends sailed back and forth looking for Dominic in the prescribed checkerboard pattern. The boat had been drifting with no one at the helm for who knows how long— five hours? Twenty minutes? They were not even sure of their position. The following week when the two friends made Ireland they telegrammed Laurence Brown in Boston, where he was doing a year at Harvard Divinity. Laurence got the job of breaking the news about their father to his sister Jeannine. She was just about to begin the freshman term at the University of Vermont.

Jeannine and Laurence spent their Christmastime in Boston that year. On New Year's Eve Laurence took her out with some friends of his to a skating party they had going. Jeannine took a fall on the ice and broke her wrist. It was the slowest part of the evening when Jeannine Brown was brought in a taxi to the hospital. Fate arranged it that Doc was the resident on duty that night. When Jeannine came in the door he knew right away what happened to her—partly from the odd attitude of her left wrist and partly because she was in stocking-feet.

While Doc wrapped this girl's pretty wrist and waited for the plaster cast to harden he had leisure to share a cigarette with her. The casualties of New Year's eve—knife wounds and the rest of it—would not start arriving for several hours; the folk tradition is that bleeding and heartache cluster near midnight, which is the no-time. Doc told Jeannine about being from Fortunes Neck, west of Springfield. Jeannine lied and told him that she had family in Springfield. Once the plaster hardened Doc walked Jeannine out of the examining room and gave her back to Laurence. He shook her good hand and wished her happy new year, and that was the end of that, as far as he knew.

A few months later Doc had a postcard from Jeannine up at Burlington saying she was visiting Springfield in the summer to see her relations, and could he show her around. That was the beginning.

Jeannine took a second year at the University of Vermont while Doc completed his residency in Boston and moved home to Fortunes Neck. In the next ten months they actually saw each other only three times—at Christmas and Easter, and once when Doc took the train up to Burlington for some big dance the college was having. They wrote letters, especially Jeannine, and it was understood that they would be married.

On the Fourth of July, 1926, Doc and Jeannine were wed in Fortunes Neck by Dr. Harris Minor, pastor of the Methodist Church. Dr. Minor later became a bit of a friend to the Weirs, whom he liked to tease as "sunshine congregants". The newlyweds honeymooned on Lake Winnipesauke. Two weeks later they came home to settle in for what looked like a sure thing.

Doc was light-hearted in those years; there was money right away. Fortunes Neck had only one other physician, a man named William Tower who had his office on Bring Street. Tower was overworked and growing old, and he was glad to send patients to a young doctor whose family was known to him.

There's certainly no crime in being well-regarded, and to be a doctor in a place the size of Fortunes Neck bestowed a light renown. Doc delivered babies, set broken bones, counseled the unhappily married, declared people dead. His practice was life in a nutshell. Doc looked the part of a Hollywood doctor, tall and Saxon with a pleasant face, and while he was at it he made a good living. He was promising and young.

In those years Doc's mother was still alive. Mrs. Weir was a solid person of good cheer. She had the burden of Doc's sister Millicent. This was how she wanted it, and she made that clear to her son.

"Your sister's my responsibility," Mrs. Weir told Doc, "for as long as I have strength. After I'm gone that'll be different."

Millicent Weir had been an invalid since the onset of

her arthritis when she was 12. By her twenties she was stuck in bed permanently, though Millicent was not so torn up by pain then as she would be later. She still had a capacity for jokes. Jeannine was fond of Millicent and nearly every day she was over to Mrs. Weir's house to visit. In most of the letters Jeannine sent to Laurence she would write, "Things are OK here."

In 1927 Mrs. Weir went to her reward. (She passed away of a galloping pneumonia, age 56.) There was no question that Millicent would go and live with her brother and his wife, and from then on Doc saw his sister's agony up close each day. He even bent the rules at the hospital and wrote a prescription for paregoric for a make-believe patient. This period coincided with Millicent's sharp decline. Pequot hospital's pharmacist, Dal Greenaway, asked to come and pray with her and Doc had no objection.

"If it does some good it does no harm," Doc told Jeannine, who was never the religious skeptic that he was. But Doc had no delusions. "What I just said," he remarked, "is a tautology."

"We play a game with Millicent and use the word 're-cover'," Jeannine wrote to Laurence, "but Doc says no one recovers from arthritis this bad. It's a wasting illness, what Doc calls the 'one-d**n-thing-after another' syndrome."

"If ever we let go of hope we all die," Laurence wrote back in reply. Even then he was a dour man, an advice-giver.

Looking back (which it is impossible not to do) looking back it can't have been surprising that one evening Millicent swallowed down all of the paregoric Doc secured for her. It might even be that she didn't know what she was doing.

That night Millicent died Jeannine was downstairs

reading. She was waiting up for Doc. About nine o'clock she heard Millicent make a sound like *Ahh*, the way people do when they can finally relax. Jeannine didn't give it a second thought until the next morning at breakfast time when she carried the tea tray upstairs.

By law Doc was forbidden to sign Millicent's death certificate, which was a lucky thing because he would have fabricated it. What a mistake that would have made. Dr. Tower worked out pretty quickly that Millicent had killed herself, as well as how she'd done it. For compassion's sake he was willing to make it officially an accident. And naturally Tower believed Doc when he claimed not to know how the paregoric came into Millicent's possession. Suspicion fell on Dal Greenaway, who stood a risk of going to jail in addition to losing his job. But there was no evidence pointing at Dal because on the Sunday after Millicent died Doc slipped into the pharmacy and stuffed the faked prescription into his pocket. He panicked, and with each day that went by it became harder to own up to what he'd done. Doc stayed mum as Greenaway was dragged through the ringer by the hospital's director in those years, Arch Cooper. Arch was the hospital's first president and he was concerned about what people would think if they heard narcotics were being stolen from the dispensary.

Arch made a call to Ronald Meursault after Dr. Tower dropped a hint that it might be worthwhile. Meursault had the title of chief constable for Fortunes Neck at this time, and given the size of the place one constable was all Fortunes Neck required. Doc was interviewed, and something about his story—something about his manner—ignited hard little doubts within Meursault.

"I know Greenaway," he told Arch. Meursault was a new cop then but had lived in Fortunes Neck all his life. "Dal makes a lot of noise about Jesus and all, which should ordinarily make me suspect him—you know, that he might be lighting up a smokescreen for some bad behavior, the way people do. But Greenaway really believes in it all, and besides I can tell you he's not stupid. If you were to ask me it might be worth pressing Dr. Weir a bit more. Unless the sister climbed out her window one night and burgled the hospital, her brother had to have got the dope for her. Had to."

Millicent's overdose was believably accidental, and if the truth had come out right away no one would have blamed Doc. Except for Arch. He was a hard case, and he wouldn't chalk it up to misjudgment or to an error of compassion. He saw in Doc a fatal failure of character, which was fair. It became Doc's judgment of his character as well.

Only Dal Greenaway ever really forgave Doc; for Dal everything worked out all right. One time he even said as much to Doc. For weeks Doc had done everything he could to avoid seeing Dal at the hospital, and then one evening they met in First Time Meats, Carlos Cooper's butcher shop on Bring Street. Dal was with his wife, and she gave Doc a bitter look. But Dal stuck out his hand.

"I'm glad to see you, Doc," he said. "These last few weeks can't have been an easy time for you. I had admiration for your sister."

Cooper stood behind his counter and watched the two of them without saying a word, not even hello. Doc knew that Dal would not have spoken to Cooper or anyone else about the business with Millicent. And yet Cooper knew. Somehow everyone knew, though they weren't sure what it *was* they knew. Just that Doc was now notorious, and by association so was Jeannine. Arch might have tossed Doc out of the hospital, even had him prosecuted. It was only owing to Arch's fear of embarrassing his new hospital that Doc was allowed to keep his job.

The Millicent story was meant to be kept quiet, but someone talked. No one knows who—people leave their prints on things in secret—but like a nervous impulse word went around of something wrong in young Dr. Weir's character. That didn't change even after he became a hero for saving everyone in the fire at Jack Parsons' farm, which was more than twenty years later.

There followed nearly 20 years of internal exile for the pair of them, Doc and Jeannine. There was something set apart about the Weir family. Eyes would always turn toward them. After the business with Millicent (as Doc phrased it to himself) after the business with Millicent Doc didn't have a friend in town but Jeannine. He had his patients and Jeannine had their two kids to raise, and they had a comfortable living. But it was a lonely existence.

Doc had occasion to revisit the business with Millicent every time he met Arch Cooper or Officer Ronald Meursault. They watched him, he felt. No one but Arch and that policeman knew all the details of what Doc had done. Not Dal

Greenaway, not even Jeannine, not really. His nearly daily encounters with Arch and the cop were Doc's affliction, a torment like a conscience that would not be quiet.

It was predictable that Doc would revisit and revisit what had been in his heart when he'd done what he'd done. Doc knew that nobody—but nobody—acts from unmixed motives. He had no doubt that he acted from concern for his sister, yet when she died he felt undeniable relief. And his willingness to let Dal take the fall shamed him. That was inexplicable.

One or two times he unburdened himself to Jeannine.

"You vitiate yourself needlessly," she told him. But Doc felt he did not. As time passed he hardened to himself.

"Vitiate?" he replied.

Doc had no friendships. He had colleagues. One man, Roger Bottle, was more cordial that the others, most likely because he had the examining room right next to Doc's so it made sense to be friendly. Besides, Millicent died five or six years before Bottle arrived in Fortunes Neck. If he heard the stories, and of course he heard them, he ignored them. They were from someone else's past.

Like Doc, Bottle was a young man of New England, conscious of this identity. He came from Portland. Unlike doc, Bottle thought he was just passing through.

Bottle was an obstetrician. He thought every doctor should want to be an obstetrician. "It makes you the bringer of life," he would say, "rather than its mere custodian. It's as close to being a woman as a man can get, I think." Bottle was gregarious, good with patients. One patient that stands out was Connie Pappas.

Mrs. Pappas worked a dairy farm in Lordshaven with her husband, Mr. Pappas. They had five children, the oldest a girl 17. Mrs. Pappas was 38, 39 when she came to Bottle; there is no record of her visit so it's impossible to know. Say it was 1933, a winter afternoon, sunny, frozen.

"I think I'm expecting," Mrs. Pappas said, not even taking off her coast as she sat down.

"Now how did I guess?" Bottle joked. Though he was ten years younger than Mrs. Pappas he was already practiced at reassuring mothers. He tipped back his chair.

"I've missed the last two months. Since I was 14 I've been regular as a clock."

"Have you had any special stress in your life lately?"

"I've got five kids. I'm married to a farmer. Milk prices are so low we'd be better selling the cows for slaughter rather than go on feeding them. Yes, I've had stress."

"Do you want me to examine you?"

"You don't need. I know."

"Any problems so far? Medical ones? How are you feeling?"

"Unhappy. The only hope I've got is some boy asks my oldest to marry him and takes her off our hands. I don't see one on the horizon."

Bottle reached for something reassuring to say but found that box empty.

"My sister told me eat pennyroyal, which you can hardly find around here. It costs so much and I've been eating it by the carload. Nothing. I'm so stupid."

"I'll be you're anything but stupid. How does your husband feel about it all?"

"We don't talk about these things."

"You're married and you don't talk about procreation?"

"No."

"Never?"

"No. He's a romantic."

For a long moment they locked eyes across the desk.

"Can you help me?" said Mrs. Pappas.

Had Bottle read a transcript of this exchange he would have had no difficulty supporting the patient in her wish, nor thought her doctor wrong if he helped her. But he was not reading about someone else. Mrs. Pappas was his patient, and he was her doctor. Dr. Bottle sent Mrs. Pappas away with an equivocation—"the law is clear, m'am, or if not clear difficult to go around unless you've a mind to, and I don't." But that night Bottle, who lived alone, theatrically paced as his obligation resolved itself. It is solemn to stop life taking root, or ought to be, even if your conscience is clear.

In Fortunes Neck there were three prominent abortionists, their names known among local doctors (one of whom took a finder's fee for referrals. His peers all knew.). The abortions these women performed were barbarous; the year before there'd been a fatal case, though no one could prove anything. If Bottle said no to Mrs. Pappas she would take her chances with one of the midwives. He knew she would. In the morning he telephoned Mrs. Pappas at her home and said he would help her.

Bottle's practical problem was that he was an amateur. He knew less about abortion than any of the ghouls he despised. On the Saturday before he met with Mrs. Pappas he drove down to Yale and revisited every text he'd ever read on

— 14 —

how to induce miscarriage. His method, ultimately, was to scrape at the wall of Mrs. Pappas' uterus with a suction curette, thinking even as he did that his ignorance was massive. In after years he was shocked by his recklessness, as is he had come at that woman with an awl. At 11, 12 weeks, whatever it was, she was barely dilated. He had only a mild sedative to relax her, and at the first contraction she flinched hard. Bottle cut her severely. Blood poured forth. Willing herself to remain calm Bottle left his patient—bleeding, crying quietly—and went next door to Doc's office. Doc had been on the telephone, and wore a look of irritation when he opened his door.

"Sorry to bother you, doctor," Bottle said, "but I have a patient next door in crisis and there's no one to assist."

Doc hung up on whoever it was (it happened to be the attorney who was drawing up his will) and hurried next door. He saw Mrs. Bottle on her back, the light in her eyes flat when she turned her head toward the two men. Doc needed no explanation. The blood on the floor beneath the table's stirrups told the whole story. Doc wondered at the miraculous abundance of gore in even a healthy woman's life.

They got to work. Bottle cleaned out the birth canal so that they could begin to stop the hemorrhaging. Into an enameled basin went clotted blood and bits of tissue recognizably human. They used packing to staunch the bleeding. Once they had her stabilized Bottle phoned downstairs and asked to have Mrs. Pappas given a bed. A nurse was dispatched by car out to Lordshaven to let her husband know she'd lost the baby.

"Baby?" he said.

After Dr. Bottle saw to his patient and assured himself that she would not die he returned to his office and found Doc with the janitor's bucket, down on his knees with a large sponge. They observed the ritual of professionals and spoke in clinical terms about Mrs. Pappas' condition, creating distance from the event. Then Bottle said, "Thank you."

"I'm glad I was next door."

"Now that it's over I've begun to tremble."

"You were calm when the patient needed you. She'll be OK. You did fine."

"I did not do fine, doctor. I'm not even completely sure I did right."

Doc nodded.

"How do women manage?" he said. He was not being rhetorical.

Like Bottle, Doc was troubled, though for different reasons. Certainly he'd been disturbed by the sight of Mrs. Pappas' abortion. Other experiences of surgery had sometimes disturbed him, too—a high-school girl's mastectomy, the removal of a boy's cancerous eye. Doc had no ethical objection to abortion; he wasn't required to have views on the subject. Medicine is made of intimacies. Doc accepted it. Once when he was home from medical school a relative mentioned a great aunt among the Weirs for whom abortion was a major line of business. "I guess we've always had surgeons in the family," Doc replied.

What Doc was thinking was that he was now an accessory to a felony, no matter if most people looked the other way. This time Doc might not only lose his license. He might go to prison.

Leaving the hospital that evening he saw Officer Meursault bent in conversation with the nurse behind the admitting desk.

"Good evening, doctor," said the policeman, straightening to his full height. Meursault's wife had recently been to see Doc with a complaint about her back. She was a big-hipped woman.

At home that night Doc thought better of relating the misadventure of Mrs. Pappas to Jeannine. Since their kids had come she'd been learning not to think about the business with Millicent. Doc preferred that Jeannine remain at ease. He was not a lovable man but he did own the basics of kindness.

Dr. Bottle never saw Mrs. Pappas as a patient again once she was discharged from the hospital. The day she went home Doc asked him how she felt about her experience.

"I did not ask," said Bottle.

Between himself and Roger Bottle there developed not a friendship but a bond. The past receded further. Then there was the big fire, when for a little while the Weir's neighbors and Doc's colleagues suspended speculation and reconsidered him.

On January 15, 1949, the temperature hit a low of 9 degrees in Fortunes Neck. That night there was six inches of crusty snow on the ground from a storm the week before. In Lordshaven, a place to the north of town, Jack and Norma

Parsons lay in bed wrapped around each other. The Parsons were so deeply asleep that they never heard the glass globe of their kerosene heater when it cracked. Flaming fuel spat on their rug like bacon fat. A newspaper Mrs. Parson had been reading when she fell asleep caught fire.

It was just after eleven and Doc Weir was driving home slowly from Pequot Hospital; the roads were glazy. A patient died on him that evening and Doc was feeling defeated. Snug behind the wheel of his two-year-old Lincoln he was glad for some time alone. Coming around a turn in Highway 12 the glare of the burning farmhouse was a terrific shock.

The time available to think things over is the distinction between terror and courage. Without a moment's thought Doc swung his big car through the gate of the Parsons' farmyard. He leapt out from behind the wheel and sprinted inside the burning house; country people, the Parsons never bolted their front door. Panes in windows and bulbs in lamps were popping in the heat. Flaming wallpaper dripped off the walls. Through the smoke Doc saw Jack Parsons, confused and choking on smoke, tugging his wife Norma in the wrong direction. Doc took Mrs. Parsons away from Jack and lifted her in his arms. Her husband he pushed forward in the direction of the door; in all the confusion Doc needed to be a little rough about it. Once they were outside he set Mrs. Parsons down on the cold path shoveled out of the snow. Her husband collapsed beside her, coughing and spitting up black phlegm.

"My little girl," said Mrs. Parsons.

Her husband tried getting to his feet but it was no good, his head was too full of smoke. "You stay put," Doc said, and with a shove he set Parsons down again on the ground.

In those days Doc was a man of some agility. He sprang up onto the porch and in one step disappeared though the blazing doorframe. In all the smoke he momentarily lost his bearings, but then through a gap in the flames he saw the stairway. He knew that would be the way up to the child. In three strides he was up to the second floor. As the burning staircase fell apart behind him Doc fell hard across the landing. Looking up he saw the little girl standing in the farthest corner of her crib. She was screaming but Doc heard no sound. Scrambling to his feet he ran into the bedroom, where amazingly there was no harm nor yet much smoke. Pulling off his overcoat he wrapped the child in it and lifted her out of the crib.

Returning the way he'd just come was out of the question. There was nothing back there now but flame and the pinched sound of snapping glass. With his free hand Doc pushed up the bedroom window and climbed out on the roof. Coatless, the girl in a bundle across his lap, he duckwalked by inches down the steepness of the roof to its edge; in a big man nimbleness is proof of spirit. Three feet below was the flat top of the porch. Beyond it Mrs. Parsons was sprawled on the ground like a picnicker, looking up. Her husband lay half in a snowbank, unconscious.

The verge of the porch was licked by flames. Gingerly Doc sat down, the child across his legs. He pressed one foot on the roof to test its condition, and it held. Without knowing what he planned to do when he got to the far side Doc stood up, arms tight around the little girl. With his first step they fell through. When Doc hit the ground he and the girl ricocheted out into the snow.

The baby was unhurt—such good luck happens all the time—but Doc had a deep cut high on his left thigh. Blood was already spreading down his torn trouser leg. He noticed this with detachment as he watched the house going up in flames not 45 feet away. He was starting to think they should all move back from the heat. The house could not have burned more completely if it had been designed to do so.

"The barn," said Mrs. Parsons.

The L, the storeroom and toolshed connecting the house to the barn, was now beginning to burn. Flame-shadows danced like a cartoon caricature of menace along its wall. Doc saw two propane tanks shiny in the firelight.

"I must have put two and two together," he would later say.

Ignoring the bloody goo on the leg of his pants Doc ran for the barn. His mind was fixed on the fifty-gallon rain barrel sitting on the roof.

In the gloom inside the barn Doc searched in panic for a ladder, but found none. Calculating the height of the haymow above him he leapt. Barely catching hold he pulled himself up. He was aware of the throbbing in his leg; the medical side of his brain estimated that he must have lost a half pint of blood. He paused a moment and computed his situation. The L was properly burning now and smoke filtered in through the walls.

There was a cathead on the outside of the loft. The yard was 20 feet below him as Doc stood upright. Deliberately he turned himself around and leaned back to catch hold of the winch. He swung his legs up over it and hung upside down a moment, batlike, wondering what to do next. It took an effort before he could twist up on the thing and stand. He pressed a hand against the wall for balance. He grabbed the lip of the roof and pulled himself up by his fingertips.

Flat against the shingles Doc needed half an instant to find his equipoise. Then he pushed up and started scrabbling toward the rain barrel.

The cistern up there was half full of slush and rimy with ice. It was a bit of a trick to leverage it in the direction of the flames creeping toward the barn, but once passed its point of resistance the thing went over on its own. Water and snow and ice flooded down and drowned the flames.

And in many ways here is where our story begins.

C ount yourself lucky if the worst you ever feel is melan-
choly. Lily Meursault was a young woman who lived
with her police-officer parents in a time and in a place where
potential mates were largely fenced off by the time a woman
was 22. If you found yourself without a partner when the
music stopped, too bad. Lilly was 25 at the time the fire happened at the Parsons farm. She was a bigger-than-average
girl, with shoulders broad as a man's. She had the sort of face
that in women is called handsome.

But there was a lure about Lily; she may as well have had
the word "fecundity" tattooed in small blue letters on one
cheek. At one moment or another all the men in Fortunes
Neck must have had ideas along that line. For years Lily was
most often seen on her motorcycle, an Indian her father had
purchased for the force in 1940. She rode in jodhpurs, preserving her from the indignity of a policeman's trousers or a
skirt, which would have undermined her look of authority.
When Lily lifted the goggles off her face and pulled the cap
off her head maple-colored hair spilled around her features
like a veil. She was no child and she understood the useful-
ness of this effect.

At 25 Lily had a sense of her landscape that was nearly
mystical; it came of so much isolation in it. When she made a
late patrol she liked to eat her sandwich sitting on the Indian
up at the Paintrock Reservoir overlooking the Mattabesic

Valley. The night of the Parsons fire she was up there at the reservoir parked on the revetment. Lily liked the inkiness of moonless nights, nights when the sky sounded like cellos. It was a frigid night and she enjoyed the cold for the way it made her feel romantic. The air was so brittle-clear that the aura of the flaming house could be seen as far away as Canaan. With her clairvoyant sense of where things were Lily knew at once where the fire would be.

Lily radioed the fire department in Fortunes Neck. She started her bike and shot down Highway 12, leaning into the glassy curves of the road. She was there a full ten minutes ahead of the firemen. The frame house had already fallen in on itself and was burning serenely. The fire ate everything but the stone floor in the kitchen.

The little girl was still wearing Doc's greatcoat. She was shaking the long sleeves, amazed by their length; speculation is a child's constant companion. Jack Parsons, in pajama bottoms and an undershirt, lay unconscious on the snowy ground in front of what used to be his house. He was shaking hard in the cold and coughing himself awake sometimes in hard spasms. There was black spittle all down his chin. Squatting by him in her nightgown was Norma Parsons, holding herself against the bitter cold as Lily roared into the yard.

Doc Weir was up on the roof of the barn.

"Come down off there, you!" Already Lily had her revolver out. She made a point in her police work of always being first to establish position.

"Not sure I know how," Doc replied. His voice was very tired. One can run on adrenaline for just so long. Doc was growing irresistibly aware of blood loss and the accompanying light-headedness. He was up there 40 feet or better, and the only way down was the way he'd come up. He didn't think that was a possibility. The ground below and the cop down there with a gun drawn were spinning around.

When Doc woke the next morning in Pequot Hospital he couldn't remember how they got him off that roof. But he recognized Lily standing beside Jeannine and his daughter Amy. He was obscurely worried because he could not recall what it was he'd told her about everything that happened.

The unconscious is a powerful thing, but *being* unconscious is neither here nor there. In accounts of the fire the Parsons family appeared only as secondary players. For some time Mr. Parsons was ill from the effects of smoke inhalation and exposure, and in any case he remembered little besides awakening to his house in flames. He had no role in the story except in the part of hapless householder. The two-year-old girl—who was called Patty—was a bad interview, and meanwhile the mother was sunk in sadness. Everything they owned was gone. Everything but what was in the barn.

DOC SAVES BARN, 3 was a story with legs. In the immediate Springfield galaxy Doc's heroics were big news. But a hero must never sing his own song; it ruins the effect. Lily Meursault would be the singer of Doc's song, and though he didn't know that yet already he disliked her for it.

Lily Meursault talked about Doc on the local radio station, WHAM.

ANNOUNCER: An ordinary country doctor, home late from a patient's bedside. A sleeping family, then fire. What happened the other night in Lordshaven could have been worse. Thanks to a passing Samaritan, it wasn't. With me is Officer Lily Meursault, who saw it all. Officer Meursault, tell us about it.

LILY: THE OTHER EVENING I'M ON PATROL. I SPOT THE HOUSE ON FIRE FROM THREE MILES AWAY. I CALL FOR HELP AND THEN HURRY TO GET OVER THERE. WHEN I ARRIVE IT'S OVER.

ANNOUNCER: IT WHAT SENSE WAS IT OVER?

LILY: THE HOUSE WAS BURNED DOWN.

ANNOUNCER: AND THE PEOPLE?

LILY: THE FAMILY WAS THERE, WHILE THE HOUSE WAS BURNED, AS I SAY. THE DOCTOR WAS STRANDED UP ON THE BARN ROOF.

ANNOUNCER: DID YOU KNOW DOCTOR WEIR?

LILY: WHEN I SAW HIM?

ANNOUNCER: BEFORE.

LILY: HE'S ONE OF THE MAIN DOCTORS IN FORTUNES NECK. MY MOTHER GOES TO HIM.

ANNOUNCER: WHAT DID HE TELL YOU?

LILY: HE WAS DISORIENTED. FROM WHAT I PIECE TO-GETHER IN THE WAY HE TOLD IT, THE HOUSE WAS A DEAD LOSS BUT HE GOT THE PEOPLE OUT IN THE NICK OF TIME. THEN HE GOT ON THE ROOF AND TURNED THE RAIN BAR-REL OVER TO KEEP THE FIRE FROM SPREADING. THAT SAVED EVERYTHING. BUT THE HOUSE, AS I SAY.

ANNOUNCER: QUITE A STORY.

LILY: I'LL SAY.

ANNOUNCER: THIS MORNING DR. WEIR, NOW FULLY RE-
COVERED BUT FOR A SLIGHT LIMP, WAS DISCHARGED FROM
PEQUOT HOSPITAL AFTER HIS FIERY ORDEAL. THE PARSONS
FAMILY—INCLUDING FATHER JACK PARSONS—ARE IN SE-
CLUSION, TRAUMATIZED BY THE LOSS OF THEIR HOME. THEY
WILL REBUILD, THEIR LIVES AND THEIR HOME. ALL THANKS
TO A PASSING COUNTRY DOCTOR.

In those days WHAM was an affiliate of the CBS radio network. CBS took the interview national. Then that
spring Doc himself was interviewed for a story about good
Samaritans in *Look Magazine*, but the little profile about him
was mainly drawn from the story as Lily was telling it. *Look*
ran a small photograph of Doc in front of the ruined farmhouse, but Lily they described as "looking like a Varga girl
on a motorcycle".

True self-knowledge might be unattainable, but ever
after when someone mentioned the Parsons fire Doc felt
the wound in his leg throb. The problem was that he had
only bits of memory, and no witnesses but the Parsons, who
weren't talking. Finally people were looking past the business
about Millicent, but Lily was the hinge on which it all hung.
Every time Doc looked up, it seemed, there was a Meursault.

Until that time, since 1926 to be specific, Ronald
Meursault had been the public face of law enforcement in
Fortunes Neck. Lily was fond of her father. It was because of
him that she was ever a cop. "It's a sweet thing," Ronald had
told her the winter before she graduated high school in 1951.

Like anyone with a family business Ronald hoped his child would keep the thing going, and being the man in charge he could fix it up.

Ronald didn't have to bring up the idea of a career in police work with Lily a second time. In addition to having conventional family feelings the teen-age Lily found her father's job a glamorous thing. From childhood she pictured herself up on the force motorcycle, the Indian, imagining herself riding to the rescue. It was a vision all mixed up with Dale Evans on a horse, although more than Dale ever was Lily was excited by the idea of being licensed to investigate the fugitive places of human behavior.

Lily's interest was also encouraged by the view of the Meursault family's social position that her father had fostered. The first Meursault, Victor, came to New England from Quebec in 1893. Victor learned to run a loom at a factory in Lynn. In 1901 he married a co-worker (a sorrowing woman named Betty O'Kelly) and they moved to Fortunes Neck. There Victor found a job in a box-making factory. Ronald was their only son, and the first of the Meursaults to be born a U.S. citizen. In 1926 he became a cop in Fortunes Neck—or rather, *the* cop.

Ronald always imagined himself a man set apart by his descent from Arcadians, even if no one in Fortunes Neck could have told him what an Arcadian was. He communicated to Lily this idea of the Meursaults as separated through unceasing indirection, as parents will. As a girl Lily took this impression and made it into an idea of her family as a priestly caste dedicated to law enforcement. Lily never knew a time when the children at her school didn't treat her differently because of who her father was. She stood out for another reason: the thing she called in her own mind "my great size".

By the time she was 12 Lily had become mindful of her height in the way other people are about an impressive nose: they know it is the first thing everyone remarks about them. In those days before girls might be admired for having big strong bodies Lily felt like an oddity. Even at 17, when she was nearly six-feet tall, it looked like Lily would never stop growing. All through school teachers regularly placed her at the back of the room with the Italian boys. Not one of them ever gave her a hard time, knowing who her father was. Early on Lily saw how her size and a cop's demeanor—filling a space with just a look—suggested possession of an advantage.

Far from shy about her height Lily made it into a defiance. As a teenager she could spin daydreams hours long in which she played the part of an Amazon, and always the beautiful queen. By adolescence she had conceived in herself a boldness about her size that impressed her schoolmates (and her sometimes worried parents) as detached sexual confidence. Which it was not. On the contrary, Lily was a long time understanding why she put off "the boys", as her mother called the whole mess of sex and the rest of it.

"The problem is you're too pretty," said Mrs. Meursault. "You were cut out for a special man, not some lunkhead who's afraid of talking to a good-looking girl. The one you get will have to be as special as you are. Don't take any less, dear." It was the sort of thing every mother says. It helped about as much as ever it does.

Lily inherited size from her mother's side; Tracie Meursault was a tall woman with straight shoulders and a square jaw. Ronald, by contrast, was never a large man until the end of his life. By then he had given up the foot patrol and was more often in his car. He blamed this change of habit for putting on the pounds.

"It's this sedimentary life we lead," he told his wife.

"Talk for yourself," Mrs. Meursault shot back. "I weigh two pounds more than the day I married you." They had a rapport like that.

One cruel thing some parents do is look to their children as the vehicle of their own redemption. It can't help but leave everyone feeling like a disappointment, and what a thing that is to carry around.

When Doc Weir's sister Millicent killed herself his wife Jeannine was seven months pregnant with their son Hodge. His parents were hoping that Hodge would be the return of their delight in life; he would let them down.

Some men never marry. After graduating Brown University in 1950 Hodge tried to follow his father into the medical profession. At best Hodge was an average student but he managed to get a place at a medical school in Grenada, the sort of place that accepted almost anyone who applied as long as they could pay the tuition. But Hodge had no gift for his studies, and after six months in the islands he was back in sunless Massachusetts.

"Hodge lacked the focus," Doc always said. To people who knew him that would always be an apt description of Hodge Weir. He had a blurred quality characteristic of actors whose names we have trouble remembering. One of those men who would look forever youthful, in spite of everything.

After his try at medical school Hodge did all right working at a paper company in Framingham. Then he came home to Fortunes Neck. Hodge went into the travel agency at the invitation of old friends from town, Ann and Robert Street.

Really Hodge came home to Fortunes Neck from loneliness, but in the funny way reputations are created he was thought to be a natural for what he called "the travel industry". He had lived in the Caribbean, he had frequented Canada for the paper company. People associated him with worldliness, almost as though he had served in the diplomatic corps.

The Weirs had another child, Amy, born in 1933. She might have done better in school than she did, but with that one defect she was a good girl in everyone's eyes. She had friends and she was pretty. Her parents gazed ahead to her future with an evident hunger. They couldn't wait for Amy to do all the expected things.

Johnny Collins caught them napping.

Something in us respects the dignity of descent and Johnny Collins had none to boast. He was born in Springfield in 1932 to a girl who worked in an office, Helen Post. His father, Robert Collins, was a man who earned his living going bar-to-bar selling hand-rolled cigarettes. When Johnny was only just an infant his mother caught a cold that became pneumonia and she died. After that Robert moved with the baby to his sister Margaret's house in Fortunes Neck. There Mr. Collins paid his way with several jobs. But then after a while he died, too, of accumulated bad luck. (The proximate cause was a van on Bring Street.) His son Johnny was left on the hands of his Aunt Margaret, really until after he left high school and entered the army.

In later life no one in Fortunes Neck could tell Johnny

anything much about his Aunt Margaret. He knew only whatever little she told him, and she told him hardly anything. "The past is past," Aunt Margaret would say if he asked questions about anything farther back than last week. Even as a little boy Johnny knew it was a dodge, a dodge that only made him the more curious to know what secrets she had. Margaret must have had a history, but she told no stories—the only person Johnny ever met who was like that. He knew his aunt moved into town only a short while before her brother Robert came to live in her house. She supported herself working in the carton factory cutting cardboard with a machine. By the time she was 40 Margaret was all but deaf from the work she did. In the spring of Johnny's last year in high school she complained of big pains in her head. She died the next summer—"joining the majority," as she had always put it—when she was only 48.

In a pretty spot overlooking the Mattabesic River, down at the bottom of Cottage Row, there used to be a Roman Catholic church called St. Catherine of Sienna. It burned down in 1943, probably because of an electrical snafu that happened when no one was paying attention. At least that was Police Chief Ronald Meursault's conclusion at the time. The fire was never investigated by an expert. Knowing the cause didn't seem to matter to any of the parties.

Two years later the charred stone foundation of the church was bulldozed to make way for the access road of the Bring Street Bridge. The bridge was completed the following year and today you'd never know St. Catherine's was ever there. It was the bridge that came to seem eternal. But when Johnny Collins was a little boy and living with his Aunt

Margaret the church was a place of spooky fascination for him. All the more so because of the three genial priests he saw coming and going all day, "up to God's knows what," his Aunt Margaret would say. She warned Johnny about those priests and about the partisans of churches generally.

"They will hollow you out," Margaret said, "and I'm not joking. They will. There's a system to it. There's a system to everything, Johnny."

Margaret never saw Johnny married. He thought she might have liked that, and he would always be disappointed that she missed it. Johnny felt he owed something to Margaret, though all his life he never knew if she had been generous in her heart toward him or merely responsible.

The Weirs knew Johnny was dating their daughter Amy two months before Aunt Margaret knew. Johnny was shy about telling his aunt—not just because he was bashful about talking to Margaret about girls (which he certainly was) but because he felt inexpressibly lucky in a way that somehow shamed him. His aunt gave nearly 20 years to raising him, and sometimes Johnny wondered if her obligations to him had prevented her from meeting a man and having a family of her own. She was a woman, after all—not a pretty woman—she looked too much like her brother Robert—but how much did that ever change anything? She must have had chances and vanities, the same as everyone. In retrospect Johnny understood that Margaret was self-conscious; she disliked having her photograph taken. Johnny used to suspect she had ambitions for height. In the few snapshots that exist she is half up on her toes and lifting her chin, either in defiance of her lack of beauty or out of a wish to appear taller.

Maybe, maybe not. With Aunt Margaret it always came down to maybe, maybe not.

Johnny was a boy the Weirs had never heard of, though they knew indirectly of his Aunt Margaret, who was raising him in the house on Cottage Row. The summer after high-school graduation Johnny was drafted by the Army and Amy Weir went up to Williamstown to start college. Johnny was destined for a post on a base in Oklahoma, so Doc and Jeannine figured that would be the end of that. Doc even drove Johnny down with Amy to the railroad station in Springfield. When Doc said so long he shook Johnny's hand with feeling.

"Good-bye for now, John," he said. "Keep your head down when you're way out west. Watch out for Indians."

What the Weirs didn't figure was that when his basic training was completed Johnny would receive a two-week leave. He took a train straight back to Massachusetts and Amy. By the time he returned to Oklahoma she was pregnant. When Jeanine and Doc found out about it a few months later they were sure that Amy had done it just to spite them. She may have.

The baby arrived a few weeks earlier than Amy's obstetrician, Roger Bottle, forecast. "Babies come when they please," said Bottle when Doc Weir told him the news. "First thing they teach you to tell the patient when you go to obstetrician school." Notwithstanding, the baby was born on the Saturday of Decoration Day weekend. She was called June, the name Amy favored. In no time at all she was Juny, and would always be.

Johnny Collins was not the best investment the army

ever made. As a family man he received more leave than the average 19 year-old private. Then in July his Aunt Margaret died, months after she first complained of terrible headaches. She died on her way to work at the carton factory, dead before she struck the curb, relieved at last of her headache. Johnny was granted ten days bereavement leave and went home to Fortunes Neck. He stayed with the Weirs; no one enjoyed it. The Weirs arranged for Dr. Minor to conduct a service for Aunt Margaret, and not knowing an alternative Johnny agreed to that. Margaret would have objected and would still be objecting if, to her amazement, there is a life after this one.

For ambiguous reasons to do with the Cold War Johnny was assigned to heating and ventilation training. He took to it. Still the army cut his enlistment short by four months. In those years the military was between engagements, and Johnny was another mouth to feed. Drafting him in the first place been just a reflex. Before Juny's first birthday the three of them were home again.

Until they had a place of their own Amy and Johnny lived at the Weirs' house, with predictable tensions: unloved son-in-law, divergent ideas on baby care, money worries. It was harder for Amy, back in her girlhood home. The Weirs were not unkind but they had no grace.

"None of this is forever," Johnny would say when Amy felt down.

Quick as they could they moved on to the upstairs of a house on Tullus Street. In the next two years they built a business on Johnny's heating and ventilation skill. With the little money Johnny inherited from Aunt Margaret they made a down payment on a small house on Cottage Row. Their happiness was ordinary.

Johnny never lost the conviction of his passion for Amy. There wasn't long enough for that. There is power in being the object of desire but there's even more in the desiring. Amy filled Johnny's thoughts to distraction as he worked all day. At home in the evenings he trailed her to the point of annoyance, telling her everything in his head the way a child would; marriage is a sometimes uncomfortable business. Johnny used to lie awake beside Amy at night thinking, "I've struck gold."

Johnny would recall that on the day of the Merchant's picnic for 1958 Amy Collins wore a red rayon scarf around her throat. It gave her neck a swanlike aspect; knowing how to dress is about having a signature style. The snapshot Johnny made of Amy that afternoon (provided to Ronald Meursault of the Fortunes Neck police and still in her file in 1964) shows Amy tall and more thin than merely slender. She looks strong, though had you seen her with her clothes off she appeared almost frail, with small breasts and her ribs showing.

We imagine the past as pale and dun, like something sinking under water, but Johnny's color snapshot of Amy taken at the picnic shows her in hot colors and carrying brilliant bolts of red and yellow cloth. Amy bought the fabric from a stall selling remnants. She carried them across her arms like firewood. She made clothing of her own design and had a small business as a seamstress that she ran out of the house. As an adult Amy's daughter Juny would remember—or believed she remembered—a dark place of mamma's things: rolls of fabric, large pattern books, wooden spools of thread, a high work table, giant shears, a smell of cloth. Juny called it "Mamma's store". The room was isolated from the rest of the house by a plum-colored portiere to give privacy for the ladies who came for fittings.

Amy left the picnic that day ahead of Johnny and Juny to go home and start dinner. Their house on Cottage Row was close enough that she could walk. Over the rough ground she moved downhill like flowing water. She moved with perfect poise—like a skater, Johnny thought as he watched her going. There isn't anyone who doesn't admire gracefulness in movement.

"Wave to mamma," Johnny said when half-way down Amy turned to look back. She smiled at her husband and her baby girl.

"Wave goodbye for now," Johnny said.

Today Juny Collins believes she remembers the Merchants Association picnic of 1958. She sees her father, a dark and partially serious young man in the green field jacket he brought home from the service. It had paint-dripped lapels. She smells frying doughnuts and feels the stickiness of cotton candy. She sees her mother walking down the hill toward home, her arms carrying the candy-colored cloth. But memory plays tricks and we can't know what they are; that's *why* they're tricks. We confiscate things we've only heard and call them ours. A psychologist Juny Collins was once urged to visit mentioned in the course of conversation that her taste for athletics represented a longing on several dimensions for a place in bed between the parents. Preposterous, even though it *is* surprising how much time people waste in life chasing the recovery of their first love.

That day of the Merchant's picnic Juny had her mother's red hair and a caramel apple. Her father held her hand and walked her from stall to stall up on the hill. A child of four more runs than walks, finding stimulation in every direction. The shopkeepers' booths ran in ranks up and over the crest of Waterhouse Hill, and people walked up and down like sailors on the tilting deck of a ship. Tillers Florist was selling bunches of flowers from a stall. Johnny said to Juny, "Let's buy heliotrope for mamma." Weak spring sunlight somewhat toasted the hillside.

It was just six o'clock when they walked home to Cottage Row. The early things were also blooming and provided a species of illumination; in heaven the evenings are like what we have down here in spring. The clocks had not yet been pushed ahead and the sky was already darkening. It was chilly now. Thunderstorms were forecast for later and ponderous clouds collected overhead. The world is irksomely full of such portents in retrospect. It makes nature seem not dumb but merely tight-lipped.

The blossoms of the big tulip tree in front of the Collins house made a kind of light. Hidden in its branches a community of birds chittered among themselves. The birds had moved in up there about a year before; they never seemed to sleep, let alone to migrate somewhere. They went on night and day, not like other birds. They were all-night singing birds. Winter and summer, snowfalls and rain, they talked among themselves around the clock. Johnny discouraged Juny from climbing up into the tree to have a look.

"Don't you like magic tricks?" he asked. "Well, if you disturbed them they would stop talking."

The soft-shaped rolls of cotton and flannel that Amy brought home from the Merchant's picnic were on a table. Johnny thought he heard Amy's footsteps on the floor above. He shouted hello up the stairs at the back of the kitchen. There was no answer. On the kitchen table was a note.

Gone for mushrooms.

Amy's canvass shoulder bag was gone. Johnny presumed she took it with her to Watermeadow to pick the mushrooms that grew for just a few weeks in the spring. In those days fresh mushrooms were hard to come by in most parts of this country, and in the month of April an edible type grew on the edge of the Mattabesic River. They were thick and meaty. Amy liked to cook them in butter, and was careful to burn them just a little. Johnny ate them greedily.

By eight o'clock darkness had fallen and Amy was still not home. Johnny telephoned Dr. and Mrs. Weir, Amy's parents. Then he called her brother Hodge, who had only been back in Fortunes Neck about a month. Finding she was in neither place Johnny went next door to speak with their neighbor Mrs. Bliss, who was just going out to walk her dog Casey. But Mrs. B hadn't seen Amy all day.

Johnny heated a can of tomato soup for Juny. After all that walking in the sunshine Juny fought to keep her eyes open while she ate. When she finished her father undressed her and put her into bed. He told her mamma was visiting with Grandpa Doc and Gramma Jeannine.

After putting Juny to bed Johnny telephoned next door again and asked Mrs. Bliss to come sit in the house while he drove down to Watermeadow and looked to see if Amy was somehow still there in the twilight. But he had no luck.

At ten Doc Weir phoned to see if Amy had come in. When Johnny told him no Doc and Jeannine drove over to Cottage Row. It isn't beyond imagining that they came to the house half hoping that Amy had left Johnny. In any baffling condition it's only human to look for the most logical explanation, and Amy quitting this marriage would have seemed logical to Doc and Jeannine. The Weirs still resisted the idea of Johnny Collins as their son-in-law. Beneath our civilized behavior simmers barbarous insensitivity; nobody's fooling anyone.

Leaving the Weirs behind in case Juny woke up, Johnny went out in the car and drove down again to Watermeadow. He shouted out Amy's name and stumbled around in the mucky earth down there with his flashlight. When he came back to the house an hour later the three adults worried in moderation until the mantle clock chimed midnight. Then they telephoned Ronald Meursault.

A motif of real life is the habit of secondary characters in one's personal dramas stepping out of the chorus, often staying front and center for the remainder of the show. At that late hour it was Ronald Meursault's daughter Lily who was working the overnight shift and answering the phone.

"I'm tied up here, Mr. Collins," Lily told him, "and my father's gone to bed." The Meursaults ran their law-enforcement operation from the parlor floor of their house on Nipmuc Street. But after Johnny explained his trouble to Lily she went to wake her father.

In those days crime was far from unknown in Fortunes Neck; there was never any golden age. Ugly things happened from time to time, but in those cases Ronald called in the Pocumtuk County police. He had sense enough to know when he was out of his depth.

About one that morning Juny came downstairs to find her father and her grandparents sitting at the kitchen table. "I heard you talking," she told them. Coffee cups and cigarettes made Juny think this was some sort of adults party, since to the extent that her parents socialized a requirement appeared to be that it take place after her bedtime.

"Where's mamma?"

As if waiting offstage for his cue Ronald Meursault rapped hard on the front door.

"Heard you got a runaway wife," he said to Johnny. Ronald may have had an idea that a joke might make these people relax, but no one laughed. Juny, though, was interested in the vision of a policeman in her house. Meursault had a .38 strapped on his wide hip.

"Most of the time it's nothing," said Meursault. "She's probably at a friend's house. You've called around?"

"Yes," said Johnny. "Everywhere. She said she was going

to pick mushrooms down at Watermeadow."

"Maybe she's still at the river."

"Not for seven hours. And I've driven over there twice since suppertime." Already Meursault's investigation had run up a blind alley. Amy Collins appeared to be more than merely overdue.

"Really technically," said Meursault, "I shouldn't be here yet. Formally a person is not considered a *missing* person until they're gone 24 hours consecutively. And after midnight we turn over all our jurisdiction to the County." As if remembering protocol Meursault picked up Johnny's telephone and called the County.

"Collins," he answered to whomever was beginning to fill out forms on the other end of the line. He took up a photo of Amy from the bookcase by the front door and described her. "Fair skin, red hair I guess, tall girl, mid-twenties. The ethereal type, she looks like." Meursault listened a moment and then asked Johnny what Amy was wearing when he saw her last. Johnny drew a blank.

"Strangely," said Meursault, "strangely he can't recall."

"I took a snapshot of her today," Johnny offered. "It's still in the camera. We can get it developed." Johnny looked at Amy's parents and saw how they were eyeing him. They found him guilty of negligence. Or worse.

"A scarf around the neck," Johnny offered. " Red. Or orange. She always wears bandannas different ways."

Meursault repeated what Johnny said into the telephone. The two men looked each other over as he spoke. Meursault was fifty-seven—not old even by the actuarial tables of his time. But he was red-faced and overweight, and he had just months to live.

About three a.m. that night the drizzle and damp that had been mulling since early evening collected itself into a steady downpour. It was the start of a four-day rain. The shower made a soothing racket in the Collins house. The thing about a spring rain is the promise in it.

Once it was evident there was nothing else for him to do Officer Meursault went home. Juny waited for someone to order her back to bed; she ostentatiously behaved herself in the hope of staying up. Her grandmother played go-fish with her. Juny thought her Gramma Jeannine was the most glamorous woman in the world. Jeannine Weir never seemed to leave the house without putting on a good skirt and some jewelry. She had a way of holding a cigarette with her left wrist bent double that Juny one day planned to emulate. There was always the scent of tobacco and perfume in her aura, and yellow teeth undermined her vanity. But to Juny Gramma Jeannine was complete in her allure.

There's a moment of inertia just before we know that a fate is undeniable. None of these people playing cards and smoking had arrived at that moment. Three times before sunrise the county cops phoned with reports of someone saying they'd sighted Amy. These all proved false alarms. It was hard on the grown-ups, but even in their worst worry they could not imagine an ending in which Amy had quit life on earth.

Which she had.

Life's worst moments have in common the trans-formation of the commonplace into something we can't stop looking at; think about that and see if it's wrong. In Fortunes Neck there was nothing more commonplace than the Mattabesic River, which for most of the year was so inconsequential that one could wade across it and barely get wet above the knees. In places the Mattabesic was nearly creek-like before it disappeared into the Connecticut River above Hartford, though it retained the formal status of river right to the end. The focus of the search for Amy Collins—the search for a body—was widespread, but instinct told them all to look close to the river.

A band of neighbors and cadets from the police academy in Springfield assisted the County police in combing the scrub at the riverbank and grubbing the river bottom with clam-digger's rakes. It rained for three days straight after Amy disappeared, but as soon as it let up they were back down to the river, poking in the ooze with sticks. Johnny Collins was among them, aware of eyes that looked his way and thought him over.

"The police are studying me," he told Mrs. Bliss from next door.

"Can you blame them?" she replied. "A disappearing wife almost always involves a husband." Johnny couldn't tell if she was needling him or offering sympathy.

It is more or less comforting to learn that disappearing is hard to do, even when it's intended. From the day we're born our lives are a trail of entanglements that don't easily let us slip away. Amy Collins' disappearance was therefore violently out of the usual, and suspicious because of that.

Juny was only a little girl and for weeks after her mother went away she saw lots of men in uniform, big pistols in leather holsters. The men went out of their way to be kind. Juny understood that this meant bad news. But children enjoy novelty and she liked the attention, still. And there was Lily Meursault, Ronald's daughter and his second in command, a woman of large frame who often pulled up to the house on Cottage Row on her motorcycle. The disappearance of Amy Collins happened just at the moment when Lily was beginning to step out of her father Ronald's shadow. Lily's role in the case was the event that fixed her as the top cop of Fortunes Neck. So much of everything depends on timing.

Lily Meursault was heir to her father's delight in a worthy challenge. Most of the investigations that came her way consisted of burglaries, wives who'd been hit across the face like Noreen Crossman or cemetery stones turned over for a prank. The biggest puzzle Lily'd ever had was the search for Amy Collins. It was what the suicide of Millicent Weir had been for her father.

In the weeks and then the months after Amy vanished an impression spread that Ronald had gotten too old and was no longer up to the job. He wore out on the long slow drags of the river and the woods. A full day of doorstepping around the neighborhoods was beyond him. Worse, Ronald seemed unable anymore to make the quick connections in his head between apparently unrelated bits of information, which is so essential to induction. People commented on that. They also noticed how Lily was the one the County relied upon in the hunt for Amy. After studying psychology at the police academy Lily understood that her father felt not one thing but several as he neared his end, ranging from pride in her elevation to humiliation at his displacement. It was the natural order, and her father knew that.

In June an editor preparing a story on the disappearance of Amy Collins for *The Springfield Union* recalled the earlier connection of Lily Meursault and Amy's father, Doc. The editor dug out the old clips about the fire at the Parsons farm in 1949. The story that ran in the *Union* was picked up by a wire service. *Look* magazine followed with a half-column article on Amy that made the connection to its feature on Doc Weir nine years earlier, the one which made prominent mention of Lily Meursault. The magazine called Officer Meursault's role in the search for Amy "a chilling irony". By such tedious accuracy a cliché acquires staying power.

It was largely the County cops who led the searches. It was given to Lily to do what her father called the house-to-house. For two weeks Lily went around with an Officer Sontag from the County force. Lily would have preferred working alone to working with Sontag; all the County cops she regarded as wall-eyed farmboys.

It was logical that Lily assumed the lead in face-to-face interviews. She was a cop who could focus, she was local and she knew all about everyone. There's much to be said about the force of personality, and Lily had that. She led the canvassing of the neighborhoods, seeing what could be squeezed from unconscious memory.

"Never be too smart to pursue the obvious," she liked to say. "Think about it and you'll always find a motive. People," she would say, "see not more than they know but more than they allow themselves to admit." Lily learned that in her psychology class at the police academy, and she never got over it.

It was late April now and the sun was climbing higher every day. On the thirteenth day of the investigation—"Lucky thirteen," Sontag joked several times, to Lily's irritation—they walked down Brook Road and knocked on the door of Helen Mercy. Mrs. Mercy was doing her spring cleaning and had all her windows flung open. Chilly spring was working its shivery magic that day, and Mrs. Mercy was inviting all of it indoors. Life was all.

Lily and Sontag spent a long time talking with Mrs. Mercy, who had been mopping her bathroom when Lily came by. She answered the door in pajamas with a kerchief on her head. Some years later Mrs. Mercy's husband Carmine would remark to his lawyer in an unrelated case that "my wife said Officer Meursault took a look and gave her the big fish eye, like she was wondering what she could charge her with."

Lily already knew Helen Mercy—they had been only

two years apart in school days. But the mask of professional-ism is assumed for good reason, and while interviewing Mrs. Mercy Lily did not acknowledge their acquaintance.

"Apologies for barging in on you," Lily said as Officer Sontag stood behind her taking notes. "You may have heard that a woman in our town has gone missing. Her name is Amy Collins. Did you know that?"

"Of course I heard. The Weirs are my neighbors around the corner on Ploughman Road. And they've had it in the papers every day—how wouldn't I hear about it?"

"What have you heard?" It was Lily's tactic to take peo-ple off guard this way, pressing them a little just to see what would happen. But Mrs. Mercy shrugged.

"That, like you say, she disappeared. Didn't she become a seamstress or something?" Mrs. Mercy owned a small dog of the yapping variety.

"That's right." Lily pretended to check her notebook. "You haven't seen her? Not back here in her old neighbor-hood, as you call it?"

"It's funny you ask."

"Funny why?"

"This is embarrassing, but one day last week I thought I saw her. That was funny in an odd way. I was thinking I should telephone someone to turn her in or whatever, be-cause I knew she was being looked for. But in the time it took me to get outside on these steps to give myself a better look she was gone."

"If you think you see her again," said Lily, annoyed, "don't waste any time phoning us."

"I don't think I wasted any time."

Lily gave Mrs. Mercy a small smile. It was meant as a warning.

"Thank you for your help," she said.

"There's one other thing. In that regard, I'm saying. My neighbor." Officer Sontag had already turned away and started down the steps. But Lily's ears twitched like a hunting dog's.

"That Saturday he was gone all day. And he never goes anywhere."

"How do you know that?" asked Sontag. Most of that day he'd been a passive member of the investigating team.

"I don't know it for sure," said Mrs. Mercy. "We were up at the Merchants picnic a good portion of that day, and I noticed that I didn't seem to see him there. Some years he goes. The reason I'm telling you," said Mrs. Mercy, "is that I think he knows the Weir family."

"What's the name?"

"Parsons. You probably remember him from when his farm burned down a few years ago."

"Yes." Nine years later that night remained an obscure source of trouble to Lily. Doc Weir might have been intrigued by this, had he known. Lily listened for something hidden in Mrs. Mercy's tone of voice.

"Mr. Parsons bought the house next door after his wife left him and took the little girl away. He works at a factory or something now."

"What time does Parsons return from his job?"

"Every afternoon at five-thirty. You'd think he was punching a clock."

You never know. Lily and Officer Sontag completed their

interviews for the afternoon and returned to headquarters at the Meursault house on Nipmuc Street. They reheated the coffee Lily's mother had perked just that morning and chatted awkwardly about the investigation and some other things; Sontag was astute enough to realize that Lily considered him a hindrance. Half an hour later they were back on Brook Road in the unmarked Ford that doubled as the Meursault family car. They parked at the bottom of the street and waited for Parsons to arrive home from his job.

Children enjoy any new wrinkles in life's fabric. It was after four o'clock on a spring afternoon and the kids on Brook Road were home from school. They all knew who Lily was, even when she was not in uniform. They gravitated to her car and asked what she was doing.

"Scram," she remarked.

The kids retreated to the opposite curb to join the stake-out of Mr. Parsons. He was not yet 40 years old at that time but was known to his neighbors as "Pop" because he lived alone.

Ever since his house burned down in 1949 and Doc Weir rescued him Jack Parsons had struggled to find a routine in the world. After the fire he never rebuilt his house out in Lordshaven. For a couple of years he was a commuting farmer, driving out to his place before dawn from a house he and his wife rented in Fortunes Neck while he tried to keep the place going, as a farm at least. But like most farmers, even before the fire Parsons lived on the knife edge between prosperity and bankruptcy; he owed more money on his place than his fire insurance could cover. He did not even have enough to pull down the ruin of his old home. Rather than look at it forever he took the place apart in pieces on Sunday afternoons for a year. Worse, Parsons felt shame— not because his house burned down, which can happen to anybody, but for having failed his wife and child when they were in danger. That made Doc Weir a better man than him. His wife Norma felt more or less the same. After two years, tired of the dark between them, Norma left Jack Parsons and took their daughter Patty with her. Parsons sold the farm to a guy who had visions of building houses on it and he sent the money to Norma. Still she wouldn't come back. Life is full of complications.

For the rest of his life Parsons led a bachelor existence and was a quiet man, permanently. As much to fill his days as for any other reason, he took a job at a plant close in to Springfield that made a specialized radio fuse for the Air Force. The routine was not a bit like farming: he worked eight hours a day and made good money. It was the steadiest thing in the world, and just the way Mrs. Mercy predicted at five-thirty on the button he turned his blue Plymouth into the driveway of his home on Brook Road.

Nothing is more suspicious in retrospect than regular habits, no matter what anybody says otherwise. Almost before he had the ignition switched off Lily and Sontag were positioned on either side of his car.

"Mr. Parsons?" Lily was flashing her badge. "Do I have that right?"

"I remember you," said Parsons.

"That's right, sir. If you don't mind I'd like a word with you, sir."

Sometimes the rough stuff need only be implied. Without showing their weapons Sontag and Lily walked Mr. Parsons into his house. Under questioning Parsons acknowledged being out of town on the day Amy Collins disappeared.

"I was at my aunt's house in Arcadia," he said. "She turned 80 that day. I can show you snapshots of myself at the birthday party. They're still in the camera."

Cops don't like interruptions and Lily Meursault was no exception.

"There's no need, Mr. Parsons." She sat facing him on a kitchen chair. Her practiced eye found photographs of what looked like Mrs. Parsons and the daughter on a table in the living room. The photos were spotted and sun-damaged.

A long time later Lily had occasion to remark to Johnny Collins that "we comfort ourselves with the belief that liars always give themselves away. Sweaty palms, won't meet your eye, a grin that won't quit. But on the contrary." Parsons showed all the give-away symptoms, but his alibi held up. The only thing that came of Mrs. Mercy's tip was a lasting case of bad blood between two neighbors.

Unofficially Parsons remained under suspicion. That same evening before fixing her supper Lily phoned his boss at the radio-fuse factory and asked him "to keep a weather eye." Parsons was fired the next day.

Memory isn't history; it's storytelling. Juny Collins trusts nothing about what she recalls of the month she spent at her grandparents' house after her mother went away; she thinks of it as a period of ice cream. She was too young to retain anything else. Uncle Hodge later told her that during the time at gramma's she often woke up yelling, and in daylight she was given to scary silences. Mrs. Bliss from next door described her as a raging id. (Not her words. Mrs. Bliss might have said "kid".)

"Picture it," said Mrs. B. "You're beginning to understand your only mamma is away forever. It's a development so strange you don't even cry about it."

For a year after Amy went away Johnny left her workroom just as it was. Then one weekend after Juny was visiting at her grandparents' house she came home to find her mother's sewing room cleaned out. The walls were painted white and the television was moved in there. Juny couldn't grasp the concept that her mother wasn't ever returning, yet she knew that her grandmother was telling her an endless string of fibs all day long.

"I spoke to your mother only just the other day."

"People go on trips."

"You can come and live with me."

"Daddy's making a surprise for you." By "daddy" Jeannine meant Doc, not Johnny Collins.

People think they are born with an instinct for knowing lies when they hear them, but as Lily also used to say, on the contrary. In children this mistaken intuition just leads to fuddlement and this bewilderment can't help but be inarticulate.

A couple of times a week Jeannine took Juny out in her creamy Cadillac to make a picnic up on Waterhouse Hill.

One day when Jeannine refused to take her to Johnny's shop on Bring Street Juny snapped the metal ladder off one of Uncle Hodge's old fire trucks and used the jagged edge to vent her grandmother's heirloom counterpane. Jeannine stitched it up, but badly so that the repair looked like a tough guy's scar. In her will Jeannine made a point of leaving the counterpane to Juny. When she died in 1979 Hodge made a ceremony of presenting it to Juny. She knew her grandmother was reminding her from beyond the grave.

It isn't really hard to work out the events that set us in motion. "Think about it and you'll always find a motive," Lily had said.

After Juny came home from her month with Jeannine and Doc she took up sleepwalking. One sticky night in July she event went out the front door and walked across the yard to Mrs. B's house. She trailed her blanket through the wet grass and dreamt of Casey barking. At five the next morning Mr. Pappas the milkman found her asleep on the front steps. He woke Mrs. Bliss, who phoned Johnny to come and get his daughter.

After Juny went sleepwalking Mrs. Bliss seemed to double her concern for Johnny Collins and his little girl. They all did. One morning Juny even heard that Uncle Hodge had been found by Mr. Black asleep in his car in front of Mrs. B's house; Mr. Black shook Hodge awake and told him, "Look, the sun is up." Her father told Juny that Uncle Hodge had been out there standing guard over the house in case she wandered outside again. She didn't believe him, she knew it was a story like the one about Santa Claus watching while she was sleeping. Still it sounded like something her uncle might do.

Johnny, meanwhile, dragged Juny's bed across the hall into his room. He put it in the far corner so the hall light wouldn't shine on her face. On a table beside it he put a picture of Amy until Juny asked him to take it away. "It makes me think of crying," she said. Otherwise they bunked together until Juny started first grade a year later.

S igmund Freud noted that for most adults the earliest
memories conserve the unimportant and the accidental. Maybe for him. Today Juny Collins saves in her head an
inventory of tiny interactions with her father in that summer after her mother's disappearance. Accurately or not, she
places most of these recollections in the evenings, when the
old life with mamma could still be invoked.

It seems to her now that she and her father spent all of
their meals alone, but that can't be so. She only wished it that
way. Juny made dinnertime hell for her father. All she would
consider eating was steak and eggs.

"Fancy tastes for a four-year-old," her father said.

"I'm almost five."

Their house always smelled of simmering things. The
only food Johnny knew how to cook was soup and casseroles.
If ever today Juny pictures those summer months the image
she retrieves is of her father sitting with her in the kitchen
holding up a forkful of something and begging her to eat.

"Have chicken," he'd say. "Mrs. Bliss made it."

"I hate Mrs. Bliss."

"Don't say hate, Juny. What would mamma tell you about
that?"

"Mamma's not here no more." Juny said this deliberately,
knowing it would pass straight through her father's heart.
Small children have no sense of restraint.

"Mamma watches over us, Juny. She wants us to be good. Eat the chicken."

"For lunch gramma gave me spaghetti and meatballs."

"You don't like meatballs you told me."

"I didn't eat any."

"Did you eat gramma's spaghetti?"

"It's like worms. No." Juny folded her arms, Mussolini-like.

Kids find fear more inexpressible than happiness; as adults it eventually gets to be the other way around. In the first few years after her mother disappeared Juny could not have told her father all that was in her skull even if he asked. And he did ask. He had his duty to Juny, and every evening he tried to make conversation.

"I want mamma," Juny might say.

"Me, too."

"When will she come back?"

"She's gone to heaven, Juny. People don't come back from there."

"Will you die?"

"Sure I will, but not until you've grown even older than I am now. I'll be around to haunt for you for quite a long while yet." Johnny was wrong about that one.

"It's stupid that people die."

"That's how it works, Juny. There are millions of babies backed up waiting to be born. After we have our turn then we make room for them." Remarkable the things that come out of our mouths.

"Everybody should stay where they are."

"You'd get tired of that. It's good that things happen. What if you hadn't been born—where would I be then? I'd miss you."

"What does 'misses' mean?"

"It means when you're sad that someone you like isn't around."

"Not that 'misses'. Like Mrs. Bliss."

"That's just what people call a woman who has a husband."

"Mrs. Bliss doesn't have a husband."

"Let's look that word up in the dictionary."

It may be that our chief source of apprehension is through our noses. Johnny's habit was to shave every evening after dinner, and he would always make a game of letting Juny search his face for any spots he missed. After shaving the skin of his cheeks glowed and he smelled of Noxzema and cigarettes. Juny liked it when her father let her stand on the tops of his shoes and they'd pretend to dance. She loved his smell of soap and fatherhood.

Twilight is the choice part of day at any time of year, better than dawn exactly because it isn't all prospect; we can begin to at rest. On summer evenings Juny and her father liked to sit on the front steps of the house on Cottage Row to see the whole show of it. It was the time when the all-night birds up in the tulip tree were at their noisiest. That tree was growing higher every season, keeping the Collins' so-called sunporch cool and damp the year round.

A child only understands good weather or bad, the way a dog does. The unseasonable heat of April in 1958 was an augury of steamy June. The air in memory was florid with wet-soil smells and the coffee on Johnny's breath and the bed of spicy daffodils beside the front steps that Amy started the year before. Johnny kept them going for quite a while after she disappeared.

"We can watch the night rise," he would say. Juny was caught by the expression "night rise"; down to this day it comes into her head at twilight. She turned her face up to the east, the full moon in the indigo sky. There was still blue daylight left in the sky but the moon was fully up above the horizon. It was so low that it appeared enormous. Juny thought she heard it making a noise, something like *ping*.

"When it's full in June," said Johnny, "they call it 'the honeymoon'."

"Why do they call it that?" Juny pictured "they" as something like scientists for the government, though she didn't understand what either scientists or the government were.

"I don't know why," Johnny told her. "Indians had lots of names for the moon. They didn't have calendars like we've got but they knew what time of year it was by keeping an eye on the moon. Can you see the face?"

"What face?" Sitting up with her father meant putting off bedtime.

"Squint up your eyes and see if you can't make the bluey spots on the moon into a face." Juny was delighted when the face came into focus for her. "That's the man in the moon," Johnny told her.

"How come it does that?"

"It's just extra. I think the moon by itself would be enough, but it's kind of nice to have it making a face at us. But if you think about it," he added, "behind everything there's a system. So I'll bet there's a reason."

Juny had no idea what her father was talking about but she liked being with him on the steps.

Once in that summer after her mother went missing she and Johnny were sitting out in front of their sunporch watching the night rise. The yeasty smell of midsummer was on the air. Juny was telling her father something about the daffodils growing next to the steps and he was smoking his after-dinner cigarette. Abruptly he interrupted.

"*Pssst*. Look!"

Johnny was pointing up into the tulip tree where the all-night singing birds lived. They were chirping their usual racket. But on a bare limb about a third of the way up a pair of jays were courting. The plump, muted female perched with regal indifference as her suitor stepped around her like a ballet dancer, e*n pointe* and with his wings spread wide. His spring feathers were luminescent, the color of the sky if it's empty. He was absolutely silent, and at the same time begging for the female's attention. Her part was to pretend not to see him, or to care.

"Isn't it great?" Johnny whispered.

All Juny saw was a couple of blue jays, her least favorite in the world of birds. They were pretty, or showy anyhow, but they were bullies toward all things smaller than themselves.

"What are they doing?" Juny whispered back. She used to like whispering.

"It's their mating dance. It's springtime and he wants to go out on a date with her."

The courting jays were still at it when darkness closed in, as if drawing a curtain on them up on that high branch in the tree. Juny went to bed half dreaming of the birds walking down a street together on their date, the female wearing a bluey cardigan across her back against the April chill, open at her throat.

Cottage Row was a quiet street of mainly older people who'd raised their children and then had those children move away; that's the way of things for us. Across the street from the Collins' house lived Daniel Potts, who seemed like an old man when Johnny was being raised by his Aunt Margaret. As a kid Johnny used to have run-ins with David Potts, the oldest boy in the family who had no friends and for good reason. When Mrs. Potts passed away in 1956 Mr. Potts was left all at sea. He was seldom seen and said little to the neighbors—he was that way even before the wife died—but he liked to go for walks in the evenings. He would acknowledge Juny and Johnny when they shouted hello.

Casey from next door was out walking with Mrs. Bliss. He hurried across the front lawns and joined them; we envy dogs their gregarious informality. Casey was a good dog and had a gift for living in the present. He snuffed at Johnny's face, at the daffodils, at the night-rise.

"Good evening, Mrs. B," said Johnny. "Sticky night."

There was always a respectfulness in the way Johnny spoke to Mrs. Bliss, as if she were more than just five years older than he. The year after Johnny and Amy were married Mrs. B bought the house next door. She was old-time Fortunes Neck, like the Weirs, but had lived in Albany, New York, for several years during the period when she was married to Mr. Bliss. She had known Amy from high-school days, when she'd gone around for a while with Amy's brother

Hodge. Hardly anyone but Hodge remembered when Mrs. Bliss was called anything by people but Mrs. Bliss.

"I find the heat relaxing," said Mrs. Bliss, "but big moons make me nervous. How are you, Juny?"

"Fine." Juny stroked Casey's back. The dog glowed with good will and banged its tail against the porch railing.

"I drove by the pond in Arcadia yesterday and saw you swimming with your gramma. Did you enjoy that?" No one talks about it, but all through childhood we bristle at the condescension of adults, who seem to think a child's inexperience means stupidity. Juny answered "Yes" politely. She wanted a dog. She and a dog could spend all day together while her father was working in his shop.

Casey hopped down and went to stand by Mrs. Bliss. He whimpered a little for her attention and poked her with his nose.

"Full moons get to you, too, don't they, sweetheart?" Mrs. Bliss looked around and chafed her arms like she was cold.

"Amy believed moonlight was healthy for people," Johnny said. "On a night like this she used to pull the drapes back from the windows to let in moonshine."

What on earth did Johnny think Mrs. Bliss would reply to that? But some kinds of longing go on and on.

Clip-clop footfalls were heard crossing the pavement of the street. They looked up and for an instant were blinded by moonlight. They saw Officer Lily Meursault coming toward them.

"Good evening," said Lily. "Hello there, Janey."

"Juny." She was disappointed that Office Meursault was not on the Indian that evening. She was thrilled by Lily in her motorcycle-riding pants and peaked hat whenever she roared up to the house on the bike, and there was always the smell of leather in Lily's aura that affected Juny happily. But tonight she had on civilian slacks and a man's white dress shirt rolled up at the sleeves.

"On the late shift tonight, officer?" Johnny was being friendly.

"I'm on the footpatrol." From the way Lily said that the others understood that she was making a police joke. "Mother's on telephones, theoretically. But she and my father are praying no one rings tonight. Sometimes they like their privacy, so I thought I'd take a walk." The Meursault HQ on Nipmuc Street was a mile or more away.

"I've got wanderlust this evening," Lily said, looking up at the smiling night sky.

"The moon causes it," said Mrs. Bliss of Lily's wanderlust. To Juny this sounded like a bad thing, like mischief, hard to reconcile with the friendly face of the man in the moon. But somehow she knew that Mrs. Bliss was playing, though she wasn't sure how. Juny was still too little to understand what it was that made jokes funny.

"I'm glad to take the air," Lily replied. To demonstrate her pleasure she sniffed deeply and inhaled. Casey watched her at it.

There's telepathy behind unasked questions, or there is quite often. Had they each been alone with Lily they might have asked her what news she had of the investigation, even Juny. They associated Lily with the power to explain the mystery of Amy's disappearance. To Juny she was becoming a familiar enough presence that her authority—combined with the scents of leather and womanliness—created maternal associations, if not affection. Today Juny finds the sequencing so obvious that she feels no need to even comment.

"Something may break," Lily remarked. She was looking at the clouds backing up overhead. "The weather will change."

At that she unclasped the red cowry-shell clip holding the brassy-colored hair off the back of her neck. Her hairdo fell around her shoulders in a manner that even a four-year-old like Juny felt like applauding. Even at that age she understood that this was a bit of business meant for her father. Some women radiate sex like a temperature zone.

"Ah, to be young again, Juny," said Mrs. Bliss. That was another joke, since Mrs. B was only five years older than Johnny and just two years older than Lily. Mrs. B was teasing, and even Juny knew it.

Mrs. B scrunched her shoulders. Full darkness had come now—night had risen—and Juny was gleeful at finding herself still out of doors and not in bed.

Lily, glancing at her wristwatch, said "I'll head home."

"Goodbye for now," Juny called. Her father always said that, and Juny loved sounding like her father. Lily turned over her shoulder and smiled at Johnny's little girl. As soon as she was gone Mrs. Bliss and Casey said good-night as well. Then Johnny put Juny to bed.

There are no unmixed feelings about anything; mixed is our condition in this life, let's face it. That summer Lily often came by the Collins house for conversation, and always in the evening. Juny didn't like it at first because she began to work out that these visits were just adults talking, and she began to know that this meant mamma wasn't coming back. But Juny didn't mind for all that long. Compassion isn't an emotion one associates with small children, but Juny learned to feel it for her father.

In Fortunes Neck Johnny Collins and Lily Meursault would later become linked together in a way that was understood to be a partnership, though no one spoke about it—or rather they spoke about it in a less than gossiping way; it would be unreasonable to expect people not to comment. Juny was the first to notice that her father was comforted by Lily, and though it made her confused in her feelings she said nothing about it. In a worried household kids learn not to rock the boat.

In October Ronald Meursault died. His heart quit and while sitting at his kitchen table he went to heaven. Lily was sorry she hadn't called good-night to him when she went out that evening on foot-patrol. She simply neglected it and afterward felt no self-reproach.

Men who imagine themselves self-educated are given to enthusiasms. Ronald Meursault was no exception. In the year before he died, for example, Ronald took up the Bible. Before that he was a believer in a practical way; all his life he called himself a Huguenot. He took up the Bible not in the pursuit of salvation but in a fit of curiosity to know what all was in it. He read through it from Genesis to Revelations. As he made headway in the book he reported discoveries to Tracie. She had grown up in an Irish household and consequently knew nothing at all about the Bible except for the outline of the plot. Anything Ronald said about it was news to her.

Ronald took up the Bible out of an interest, not out of some late-in-life pursuit of solace. Too bad. He could have used some solace in the last months before he died, just as Lily was coming into her own. Ronald was just turned 57 and could not pretend anymore that he would be a cop forever. He was a cop for so long that he assumed people would always look to him for aid, or look away from him if they were up to no good. He seldom had to be brave in his job but in the course of even an ordinary day Ronald had to show degrees of strength or prudence. He loved the challenge of finding the balance of these qualities. Now the thing that gave him a reason for getting out of bed in the morning was ending.

On the last night of his life Ronald was in the kitchen with his wife. Tracie was washing the supper dishes while her husband sat at the table reading the Bible. Ronald was the sort of reader who liked to share aloud a good bit when he came across one. As he often did that summer he was reading out something he'd come across in the Old Testament.

"Get this, Trace," Lily heard him saying. "It's in Judges. 'And when he was come into his house, he took a knife, and laid hold on his concubine, and divided her, together with her bones, into twelve pieces, and sent her into all the coasts of Israel.' What can anyone have done to deserve a demise like that? The Bible never says. It just tells you something happened. And I'll bet this guy gets away with it."

"Sounds like a poor job of police work among those Israelites," said Mrs. Meursault.

"It doesn't mention what they did for law enforcement,"

Ronald replied. "You'd think they'd want it, since all they ever seem to do is hit each other on the head. From what I'm reading that seems to be the whole story with them."

Ronald left this life in a way he would have wanted. For several years he had been the protector of Noreen Crossman across the street. Noreen's husband Bill was a son of a bitch. No one but the Meursaults knew this, though, or knew it in detail the way they did. It was Mrs. Crossman's private trouble, and the Meursaults respected her right to it. Then one afternoon Mrs. Crossman came across the street with a purple shiner on her eye, and she gave Tracie an earful.

That night Ronald waited up on his front porch for Bill Crossman to wander home from the Bring Street Café. About two a.m. Crossman came down Nipmuc Street whistling the *Rose of Traleigh*. Ronald appeared to him from between two parked cars and said, "I hear you like to hit people, Bill. Hit me."

Before Crossman could open his mouth Ronald had clubbed him to the ground with his flashlight. The bulb broke, he cracked him so hard.

Ronald bent and spoke to Bill in a whisper.

"I can charge you with assault and make it stick, Bill. But in jail you'd be even less use to Noreen. You better go somewheres far away. Once you get a job start sending your wife most of your paycheck. Or otherwise I'll come after you."

Crossman went to live in Framingham—"the city of ne'er do wells" Mrs. Meursault called it, though Lily never knew where she got that idea. Forever after Ronald was a hero to the Crossman family, and Noreen would often stop him to ask advice on all kinds of things—even about home repairs, about which he was illiterate. Lily's mother didn't like it.

"You watch out for that one," Mrs. Meursault told Ronald. "She's got bait in the water."

"The woman's got no one to talk to, Trace. She's always looking over her shoulder for that rat to come back around again."

"Never mind," said Tracie. "I know what I'm talking about." She wasn't half joking. Nothing happened though.

Bill Crossman came back the night Ronald died. With the twitching antennae of an aging detective Ronald knew something was amiss about nine o'clock. He hurried across the street and there was Crossman rattling what used to be his front door. He was trying to express something about his ownership rights in the house and by extension in his family. Bill was a little drunk and that made it easier for Ronald to grab him by the lapels and waltz him out into the street. The Crossman children appeared in the doorway to watch as Ronald spoke softly in Bill's ear. Whatever it was he said must have frightened Crossman so much that he was never heard from again.

A good thing for him too, because Lily Meursault would later make the connection between this exertion and a few hours later her father's heart giving out.

Lily would like to think her parents got in one last roughhouse that night; that's what they called it. Ronald would surely have felt invigorated by his skirmish with Bill Crossman. In any case the next morning when her mother came downstairs early to make the coffee she found Ronald dead. He was sitting at the kitchen table in his pajamas with a piece of pie on a plate in front of him.

B y the end of autumn all the obvious steps had been taken in the search for Amy Weir. Sometimes there were "sightings" reported to Lily, but these were only ghost stories. Three different times Mrs. Mercy phoned to say she'd seen Amy walking down Brook Road; Lily began to regard Mrs. Mercy as a nuisance.

Even Johnny thought he saw Amy once. It was a Saturday afternoon. He came in the house and saw Amy bent over her worktable in the sewing room. She was putting a button on his winter coat. But when he went in there he found nothing, nobody. He went to the hall closet and hanging there was the coat, one button missing since the winter before. For the rest of his nights the scene repeated as a recurring dream for him; it's not at all uncommon to acquire new archetypes for the unconscious late in life. Each time Johnny woke from this dream his desolation was epic.

Johnny understood that the hunt for Amy was effectively abandoned by the time the leaves changed color. Loved ones don't always know when they're licked, but he did. Amy gone from the world was growing on him as a fact.

On a sunny Sunday afternoon, which in Juny's memory is imprecisely associated with Halloweentime, Johnny raked leaves in the backyard of the house on Cottage Row. He was saying little in reply to the things Juny said, and while she understood that this was not the same as irritability her feelings were hurt by it just the same. Her father's thoughts were far away from her. She felt like nobody.

The air got colder as the autumn light flattened out across the backyards of Cottage Row and Sycamore Road, one street over. It was the hour of pinking in, as they used to say. Juny watched Mrs. Bliss next door burning old clothes in a bonfire. It was a cold day and smoke from the fire hugged the ground. When Mrs. B poked at it sparks flew up. Juny found a stick and beat with it on the chain-link fence between the two houses. The sound of pinging metal bounced around the yard. It drove Casey wild.

Juny got hungry.

In October life buttons up, infusing even the best of us with a shade of sorrow; it is not unpleasant. From the back of the Collins' house the sun sank behind the cloud ranks that were drifting like fat balloons over the Lordshaven Ridge on the far side of the Mattabesic. Well after it was gone from the sky the sun left its light behind—traces of alternating iridium and red, stacks of afterglow. Hard to believe heaven doesn't circle around us.

Johnny crouched by his pile of leaves to watch. Juny turned her eyes from the light in the sky to her father to the light; this created the optical effect of a blue aureole around him. Juny liked the trick and went on doing it until she was bored. Holding her stick she went and stood over her father.

"Daddy," she said.

Johnny looked up at his daughter like a man waking. The blankness of his eyes dissolved and he concentrated himself. Dusting the seat of his pants he straightened up. He was trying to smile as he walked Juny into the house.

"Well, dear," he said, "now it's just the two of us. Let's have soup tonight."

Johnny Collins had the gift of a born mechanic for seeing into systems and after some reflection understanding what made them go. As a result Collins Plumbing & Heating got calls beyond garden-variety clogged drains and dripping faucets. In September, 1958, Johnny got the biggest payday of his life when he won the sub-contract for the heating-and-duct work at a residential development that was going in out in Lordshaven. The day he got that good news Juny started kindergarten; events are just relentless.

In that same month Johnny got a call from the Massachusetts fish and game commission, which had a hatchery up the Mattabesic River. The water-aeration system they used to keep the fish happy was clogged and the tanks were deoxygenating. The Mattabesic was such a silt-laden river that the intake pipe often clogged with mud. This time the blockage was so bad that nothing would clear it. Johnny's solution was to rig a diverting pipe while he mucked out the main. What he found at the mouth of the agitating pump made his heart stop: a plug of sodden women's clothing. The hatchery supervisor was standing beside him when Johnny found it. He could feel what the other man was thinking. There was a sundress and a pair of white panties—summer clothes, and for a woman with a larger frame than Amy's.

"Probably belonged to some swimmer who went home

naked," Johnny said as he extracted the clothes in ripped wet strips.

"I'd've liked to seen that," said the other guy. Even after the clothes were removed the intake filter was impossibly snarled and had to be replaced.

For better or worse sadness concentrates us. One could see that in Johnny's face as he went about his day. Everyone knew his story. In the weeks and then months after Amy disappeared people asked the same questions and gave the same consolations all day long as he went about his work. They felt a mix of compassion and of course their own curiosity.

Then two years passed. Life went on and people had their own problems.

We are born yearning and as time goes on it only gets worse. After a year and even after two there was a specific hunger for her mother burning in Juny. She spent those first two years just waiting for the time to be over, hoping whatever had happened to her mother was an episode, the truth of which was a secret meanly kept from her. Juny was half convinced that her father was still in touch with her mother. Between her father and her grandparents, between her father and everyone, Juny heard the purring of things hidden from her in adult conversations.

Children understand the meaning of soft voices. It is the sound of things kept from them. Juny noticed how voices dropped when she entered a room and smiling faces turned her way. After being put to bed at night she lay awake for what seemed like hours and listened hard to the grown-up noises of dishes washed, telephone calls, chairs scraping. She made guesses about a parallel world. When we are children we suspect our parents of many secrets in the ties they have apart from us. This is our first taste of status anxiety, finding out that we must share affection; what a disappointment.

Juny's little skull held an anthology of recurring dreams to do with Amy, whose face she now barely remembered. In one of these dream she and her mother stood across the street on Cottage Row in their nightgowns watching families move in and out of Juny's house. The new people came and went in sped-up time like an old silent movie. In another dream she saw the form of a woman lying face down in an unmade bed. She would shake and shake the figure to wake up whoever it was, but it never would. These repeating dreams were sort of sad, but whenever they began running in her head the sleeping Juny half welcomed them for the chance to be with her mother.

If the unconscious made noises they would be the sound effects of old-time radio—locks turning, doors opening, doors closing. Locks turning and doors closing were often heard in Juny's house. Once in a while there was talking after she came to bed, voices that merged with her dreams, but they were never her mother's; Juny had no memory of how her mother sounded. But there *were* voices, noises—not of her mother but of someone, and like weeping.

"Do you have fun with Mrs. Bliss?" Johnny asked over

supper one evening. This was in an interval when Mrs. Bliss was being paid to mind Juny after she came home from kindergarten in the afternoons.

"Yes," she said. In fact Juny was miserable with the arrangement. Unlike her Gramma Jeannine, Mrs. Bliss had no talent for children. Even people who liked Mrs. Bliss called her "wry," and that's a quality wasted on a five-year-old. Mrs. Bliss had eyes you couldn't see behind, wide eyes the color of shiny walnuts, eyes like what a horse has. Juny noted a horseshoe Mrs. Bliss had nailed over her front door and imagined some connection. When she asked about it Mrs. B said the horseshoe was to keep devils from crossing her threshold. She made jokes like that.

"Today what did you do?" Johnny asked.

"Went in the car with Casey."

"Where'd you go?"

"To get the rent."

Often behind the screen of convention is a life of economic improvisation. Anyone who knew Mrs. Bliss found it hard to say how she paid her bills and kept a roof over her head. It was somehow known that she received a regular payment from a former employer in Albany—money that was not quite a pension; after all, she was only in the neighborhood of 35 or so in this period when she was minding Juny. Her family had deep roots in Fortunes Neck. (Mrs. B's maiden name was Cooper. Until his passing in 1950 her father was the local butcher.) When she was 19 she married Mr. Bliss, a man from Springfield about whom people recalled little except that he had been too old for military service during the war. It was after she married that Mrs. Bliss moved to

Albany. Four years later, in 1953, she was back home. Judging by the evidence she was a divorcée.

It was through Mr. Bliss, whoever he had been, that Mrs. Bliss acquired a pair of properties in Lordshaven. How this came about she never said. The two shingled houses were typically rented by single men or the recently married, usually for just a year or so as they waited for something else to develop. The properties provided income for Mrs. Bliss but hardly made her prosperous, not in any visible way. When Johnny Collins offered $35 a week to look after Juny he had an idea she'd be glad for the money. He had noticed how she kept a clean house.

At first Juny found Mrs. Bliss more entertaining than she had hoped. Mrs. Bliss had a steady flow of things to relate— what is this impulse to review history? One day when it was spring, for instance, they were out on the road in Mrs. B's round grey Pontiac to collect the rents in Lordshaven. Casey was with them. The road out there from Fortunes Neck took them past the ruin of the old Parsons farm. As they drove past the place Mrs. Bliss pointed out the stone foundation of the old house.

"A long time ago," she said, "before even I was born a young man lived on that farm with his mother. They were there by themselves because the father had gone off."

"Where did he go?" Juny asked.

"Who knows where they go?" Mrs. Bliss replied. "But one day the young man met a girl at church and fell in love with her. The boy told his mother that he was going to marry this girl. The mother cried to hear that she was losing her son. She cried and cried, and she was very mean and made up bad stories about the girl that she pretended other people said."

"That's lying." Juny was hardening in her impression of mothers as a category of floating character. Beside her in the backseat was Casey. As the car sped past the forlorn farmstead Casey watched out the window.

"You're right about that, Juny. The woman made her son so angry when she lied that one day he moved out off the farm and went to Fortunes Neck to marry the girl. A little time went by and the son had a visit from the hired man the mother paid to help with the farm. 'Your mother is sick,' he said. 'Please come visit her.'" Mrs. Bliss used a funny whiney voice when she told this part. "So the son went out to the farm to see her, but after that for a long time no one saw him again."

"How long?" Juny asked. Perhaps there was a standard duration to these disappearances. Hope fluttered.

"Months and months. Until after the winter when the snow melted."

"Where was he?"

"In New Hampshire. The boy was found tied up to a tree and he had died. They only knew it was him from a paper he had in his pocket. After they found him the hired man came to tell the mother, but when he went to the farm he found the mother on the kitchen floor. She had died too. You can still see that kitchen floor from here—see? Sticking up in the field." Mrs. Bliss pointed. "Looks like a place for dancing."

Histories of the early years anywhere are saturated in violence and surprise; whatever Edenic interludes there may have been are only there for contrast. By age six Juny was as

inured to stories of bloody murder as most kids, which is to
say intermittently. The tale of the young man and his mother
was disturbing to her, and it frightened her that she could
not say why. In a way she couldn't say this feeling was connected to dreams she'd had about her mother in which she
was calling but made no sound.

"For years no one went near that place." Juny wished that
Mrs. Bliss would stop telling this story because she could not
stop listening. "After a long time some French people came
and bought it. But then it didn't rain for almost two years,
and then the Frenchman's wife got cancer. So they moved
away to where the wife could be and then Mr. Parsons had
it for a while. Did you ever meet Mr. Parsons, that fella your
grandfather saved from burning up that time?"

"No."

"Well, he did. That's why that farm is abandoned like
that." The way Mrs. Bliss mentioned this Juny wasn't sure if
somehow her grandfather wasn't to blame for the farm burning down. It's surprising in retrospect that Mrs. Bliss didn't
bring up any more about the story of that night and what
happened to Jack Parsons and all of it. Mrs. B knew about
Parsons and she wasn't the type to leave anything out. But
she was not a gossip because she never said anything con-
sciously mean. She just liked sharing these things.

Certain moments stay in us forever, like strontium-90.
Forty years later Juny can still see Mrs. Bliss at the wheel
of her car, spring sunshine on the leafless tree limbs, Casey
taking it all in with a regal disinterest. When she thinks of
it now the tightness comes back in Juny's throat exactly as it
did that day, the tightness before tears.

"Did I say something to frighten you, Juny?"

"No."

"I didn't mean to make you scared, pet."

"I'm not."

Silence can mean all sorts of things, including the absence of anything to say. For days Johnny noticed that his daughter barely spoke a word and wouldn't eat much of even steak and eggs. He asked Juny what the matter was so often that at last he made her cry. But she told her father nothing about the farm with the curse on it.

Soon after, Juny was spending the afternoons with Gramma Jeannine. That arrangement continued until after Juny began first grade, when she started spending afternoons in the care of Miss Most at Collins P&H until Johnny was ready to close up.

Still, Juny remained chummy with Mrs. B. She was often next door at her house playing with Casey, half hoping that Mrs. Bliss would tell more things that had happened, half afraid that she would.

One reason for having children is the inflated importance they assign their parents. Collins Plumbing & Heating, for example, was not the only such business in Fortunes Neck. But it was the only one with its premises on Bring Street, the town's main stem.

To quote Robert Frost, the past is made simple by a loss of detail, and early memories qualify as that sort of past. Juny remembers her father making house calls, like a doctor. In girlhood she imagined him as an indispensable man of the community, a peer of the fire chief and the mayor. (She was only imagining a mayor. Fortunes Neck was run by a board of supervisors, but how could she be expected to know that?) Juny believed the whole town held its breath until her father peered down a drain with his flashlight and said, "Let's see what we got."

Johnny Collins was a one-man band, if you don't count Carol Most answering the telephone and doing the paper-work—aspects of business for which Johnny had no taste. The phone rang and Miss Most answered, "Collins P&H." Juny loved the idea of the abbreviation, which she associated with the big time. She responded to the smell of her father's shop. As a grown woman specific odors—oil on dust, solvent, hot metal shavings, stewed coffee—still bring back not just the memory but the sensation of that place.

We win our freedom by degrees and Juny was slower than most of her schoolmates to get the freedom of her neighborhood. Her father arranged his calls every afternoon to be there at her school at two-thirty when classes got out. There was one time when his car died out in Lordshaven and Miss Most picked Juny up instead. Juny liked Miss Most. She was a plain woman with sour breath. But she was kind to Juny and somehow managed to run the little office at Collins P&D and still give Juny an ear when she described her day at school. And apart from talking to Miss Most all Juny could do in the shop was her homework or read a book. Usually there was coffee cake.

In the winter, when night rose early, Juny was impatient at the shop after school waiting for her father to finish so that they could go home. Sometimes she liked to go outside and stand on the sidewalk from where she could look in at him. She enjoyed the theatrical illumination of her father under the bluey green fluorescent lighting hanging from the ceiling. She liked the idea of watching him when she didn't think he knew it. He bent over his bench with a concentration she later learned to call pious.

Saints are friendly, we imagine, if not thrillingly so. Juny was briefly sent to Sunday school under pressure from her grandparents, and when she heard about saints she projected her father's worthiness on all of them. In her mind's eye—an expression she loved—in her mind's eye Juny even dressed the saints somewhat like Johnny, not in flowing robes but in his green khaki pants and shiny corduroy shirt—male or female saint, it made no difference. To Juny the outfit of purposefulness was the work clothes her father wore every day as if they were a uniform.

The study of divine illumination must be fascinating. Today, for example, Juny realizes that it was during this period that her father was becoming holy. Holy in the way he swept out of his life everything but what was essential to looking after her and preserving whatever of Amy still lived in the house. Holy in his tremendous concentration. This conviction grew in Juny with every year that passed.

D aniel Potts lived across the street from Johnny Collins ever since Johnny was brought to live with his Aunt Margaret on Cottage Row as a boy. Mr. Potts died in the hot July of 1961. Within a month of the old man's death his son David unloaded the house on Cottage Row at a bargain price, just to be rid of it. He sold it to a woman named Diane Horn, whose divorce was finalized in the very week she bought the place. The same lawyer handled both transactions for her.

On the day Mrs. Horn moved in Juny was in front of her house watching the men unload the long van. She stood on her curb with the dog Casey stretched out on the green grass behind her. When Mrs. Horn spotted Juny watching she waved. Mrs. Horn had a little girl of her own, whose name was Irene.

"Go make friends," said Mrs. Horn, and she gave Irene a little push.

"Is this your dog?" Irene asked Juny. Irene stroked the top of Casey's skull. Irene wore tomato-red shorts.

There are children with an appetite for their parents' stories and an eagerness to understand past times. Why the past? It's in the electricity of things in plain view and still strange. Juny had this taste for past things. She lived with a belief that things were always happening over her head, and she was listening all the time for chiming facts and coincidences. To this day she has a fascination with old coins, for instance. She goes through her change compulsively checking dates. One day not long ago she found a nickel in her pocket minted in 1939. She was pleased about it for days.

Juny liked it when older people told their stories. Her new friend Irene Horn could not have cared less that the world was not baked fresh every morning. For her, existence was perpetually blossoming and had no platform in history. She was a seven-year-old romantic.

Irene was Juny's first best-friend. On Cottage Row they were the only kids of their age, and except for bedtime they were together all the time. Every morning that summer after Irene moved in they stepped out their front doors almost simultaneously at eight o'clock, as if on a signal. They met in the street and began to improvise their day.

Most times they ended at the far end of Bring Street up on Waterhouse Hill. At the top of the hill there was a copse that the girls imagined as a house, a house on the edge of some all-purpose frontier. Irene made up a game called "Orphan". The game had a floating set of rules, but mainly it required that Juny and Irene be sisters living alone on their own. Something horrible had always happened to their parents—Apaches, Redcoats, outlaws, Nazis or whatever it was Irene had watched on television with her mother the night before. The girls took turns being big sister and little sister. Big sister had authority but the role of little sister offered wider scope for dramatization. No matter which part she played Irene always put on the same voice, part Scarlet O'Hara and part Ma Joad.

BIG SISTER (*PRETENDING TO IRON CLOTHES, SIGHING IN RESIGNATION AT HER ENDLESS LABOR*): BETTER BRING THAT CAT IN. LOOKS LIKE RAIN'S A-COMIN' ON.

Little Sister: THAT DARN CAT KILLED A MOUSE THIS MORNING AND DRAGGED IT IN OUR HOUSE.

BIG SISTER: THAT'S THE REASON WHY WE HAVE TO HAVE A CAT.

LITTLE SISTER: I FELT SO SAD FOR THE POOR MOUSE. HE WASN'T HURTING ANYBODY. *(SHE PRETENDS TO CRY.)* WHY DID THE CAT HAVE TO KILL IT?

BIG SISTER *(HOLDING THE OTHER IN HER ARMS):* IT WAS A MOUSE, DARLIN'.

There were certain riffs they liked to play over and over, and anything to do with cats was a favorite. Juny found cats boring but Irene thought they were noble, and like spies. The girls' invention never failed and the story lines just piled up. In later life Juny was still capable of losing herself inside her imagination, but such moments were trance-like and solitary. With Irene everything was a collaboration, even the silence.

That summer Irene introduced Juny to movies. Johnny and Juny had a television set in their house but they almost never turned it on, and as a result Juny never learned the habit. But across the street nearly every night Irene and her mother found some picture to watch on TV—the *tee*-vee, Irene called it. They watched with all the houselights down to simulate a regular movie theater. From her bedroom window Juny looked out across the street for the phosphorous light of their television, the private blue glow within Irene's house.

Irene and Mrs. Horn had indiscriminate taste. *The Crawling Eye, A Fever in the Blood, Robin Hood, Big Deal on Madonna Street*—they'd watch anything. Irene would see a film one night and the next day be able to recite whole swaths of dialog. In that way Juny sometimes found her wearing, though they were friends.

Irene's mother was a pretty if off-centered woman who would never make many friends in Fortunes Neck. She was too quick to unburden herself.

"Marriage burned me for life," she told Mrs. Bliss the first time they spoke. Mrs. Horn spoke in staccato jabs, like an equivocal boxer. She was still young then, perhaps not even 30, and attractive. She was tall and dark-haired in a way that Irene said reminded her of Patricia Neal.

A few days after Mrs. Horn moved into Mr. Potts' old house Johnny went across the street to introduce himself. Mrs. Horn responded to Johnny's sympathetic nature and her story poured out.

"Marriage burned me," she told Johnny. "Eight years ago when we got married he—my husband, 'the boy', I call him now—couldn't get enough. He loved me, he loved me, he loved me. Love, love, love. When we met he put himself over as a nice, happy schoolteacher. After about three years of that—naturally it's after he has a daughter to consider—he decides for himself that at heart what he really is is a serious musician. In other words so he could play the piano all the time. I can't tell you where he ever got that idea. Not from anyone who ever heard him play, that's for sure. The ginmills in Framingham wouldn't even let him play the piano for free, that's how terrific he was. From there I don't have to tell you that it got to be a source of argument between us, which as you can guess wasn't good for the atmosphere in our home, so now on top of everything I was worried about Irene. Then eventually about a year ago the inevitable happened and he met some dame who was willing to fan the flames of his delusion. When I found that out, I can assure you, I didn't even wait to discuss it. You don't have to imagine the rest, Mr. Collins."

Mrs. Horn remained in the hell-hath-no-fury frame of mind for a long time; it's possible that she remained in it forever. Johnny would always keep his distance from her because she pulled at him with such unhappy gravity. It should not be surprising that to her daughter Irene *Crack in the World* and *Duel in the Sun* were equally fantastic.

Right away that first summer after she and her mother moved to Cottage Row Irene went through a phase of asking every adult she met how they'd come to know their spouse— not to excavate the past, as Juny might have wanted, but to clear up some things. The easy explanation for this curiosity was that it was something to do with her parents' divorce, some idea she was hammering on within her seven-year-old psyche. But she was so persistent in her curiosity that it was as if she were pursuing a research project; in an adult it would have been called just nosey.

Older people told Irene surprising things. It was because she knew how to be adorable; Juny was wise to the scam even if the adults were not. Juny understood that around children grownups say more than they imagine, believing kids are oblivious to all but the surface of things. As Lily Meursault used to like to say, on the contrary.

Irene asked Doc for the story of how he met Jeannine. It was Labor Day and Gramma Jeannine was up in Vermont visiting her only brother Laurence. Probably out of loneliness Doc asked Johnny and Juny to come by his house for a cookout. Juny asked her grandpa if she could bring her new friend along.

"I've seen your mother at the hospital," Doc said when he met Irene. "She's very ingratiating."

"Thank you," Irene replied. Cunningly, she admired a formal photograph of Jeannine that was hanging at that time in the hallway of Doc's house. That was her entrée to ask what he remembered of the first time he met his wife.

"I always say Jeannine started out as a patient of mine and she's been patient with me ever since." We all enjoy puns but they aren't like riddles in which something useful to know is embedded. Irene pressed Doc for detail. "Well," he said. "Well, it was 1924. Jeannine was down in Boston for Christmastime visiting her brother Laurence. He was at Harvard Divinity that year and Jeannine came to spend the holidays. On New Year's Eve Laurence took her out with some friends of his to a skating party they had going. Anyhow, Jeannine took a fall on the ice and broke her wrist, and when they brought her in to have the wing mended I was the guy on duty." Doc was drinking Manhattans that day.

"The way they learn you in medical school I rotated the wrist a little, and from the way she yowled I knew my conjecture was correct." Doc paused for a laugh but the girls didn't realize he was joking. They thought he was giving the elements of his diagnosis. "I took an x-ray anyhow, just to give us both the experience of radiation. I knew she'd be fine in a few weeks. Her only problem was that she was left-handed. I joked that until the crack healed she should find some handsome football player to take notes for her, and when I imagined this lunkhead off the gridiron I noticed a twinge of jealousy. All of a sudden."

"Did you fall in love then?" Irene had no idea what the phrase meant. Perhaps she asked the question hoping someone would define it for her. But in the clichés of romance the truth remains hidden.

"Of course not," said Doc. "I never expected to see this girl again. What would have been the good—eh? She was sure pretty, though. To me she looked like Claudette Colbert, an actress in the movies then that you probably never heard of."

"I saw her in *Bluebeard's Eighth Wife*." When it came to motion pictures Irene was a child savant, and such outsized knowledge in a peewee girl made Doc laugh. Juny, meanwhile, had no idea who they were talking about, though she understood that they were comparing Gramma Jeannine to someone beautiful.

Juny was several steps behind in this conversation overall. She was still chewing on the image of her grandmother iceskating. The idea wasn't beyond possibility. Jeannine Weir could have been said to look the part of lady-athlete, one in retirement, in the same way Doc looked the part of smalltown physician; it was something about their angularity. The thing was, though, that Gramma seldom seemed to move. Juny equated this stillness with elegance.

"Were you hoping you would see her again?"

"It wasn't like that, like storybooks. I walked her out of the examining room and gave her back to Laurence. Anyhow, I shook Jeannine's good hand and wished her happy new year. That was the end of that, far as I knew. Then a few months later I get a postcard from her up at Burlington saying she was visiting Springfield in the summer to see her relations, and could I show her around. You could say that piqued my interest." Doc looked likeable when he smiled.

"It was *then* I fell in love," he told Irene. "I liked her forwardness." This was his punchline.

Grandpa Doc was born with the Weir name, which let's face it had no currency beyond Fortunes Neck. Even after his sister Millicent's suicide Doc had his family and he had his medical practice. He earned a good living from his practice at Pequot Hospital, which provided a variety of comforts. Then later he was a hero for a while after the fire at the Parsons farm. He was known for being notorious, although for reasons that people were beginning not to remember—until, of course, his daughter disappeared.

On his own Doc's son Hodge had what he had: his surname and his easy nature, and these looked at first like a good start in life, especially after returning home to live in Fortunes Neck. Fairly often Uncle Hodge was over to visit on Cottage Row, and if he was around he was always willing to play games with the girls if they asked—jump-rope, anything. From his desk in the window of the Globetrotter travel agency on Bring Street Hodge waved at them if they were walking home from playing orphan on Waterhouse Hill. Hodge waved to anyone if they waved in at him.

Hodge Weir was 33 in 1961, and that he should be single at such an age made him an object of intense interest to Irene Horn. When they were older and teenagers together Irene once confessed to Juny that her first crush had been on Uncle Hodge.

"I thought he had the sweet personality," she told Juny.

In the words of his old school friend Mrs. Bliss, "Hodge had panache." In their school days Mrs. B had been in the same class as Hodge. One time she showed Juny and Irene two pictures from her high-school yearbook, in one of which Uncle Hodge was dancing. In the photograph he appeared to be executing some sort of private adagio. They were attendants in the court of the prom's king and queen at the senior prom in 1946. The yearbook photo showed them at the back of the retinue—Hodge in his bandleader's tuxedo and Mrs. B in a shiny floorlength dress. In the picture their hips look connected but their heads were tipped away from one another. The anxiety of adolescence was all over their faces.

"He looks like Bobby Van," said Irene.

"That's exactly what I was always telling him," Mrs. B replied.

To Juny and Irene the picture only confirmed that everyone above them had always been grown up. It was interesting to see that they used to dance. It was hard to picture Hodge dancing, or Mrs. Bliss or any of them. But everywhere people dance. Dance naked, dance in tweed. Dance like kangaroos or gorgeously.

In the old days Mrs. Bliss and Hodge went around in

the same gang of kids. Back then Mrs. Bliss had the last name of Cooper. Like the Weirs, the Coopers had a connection to Fortunes Neck that went back a long time. The family legend was that one of their ancestors helped chop trees on Waterhouse Hill. When Mrs. Bliss was growing up her parents had a butcher shop at the end of Bring Street nearest the Hill, First Time Meats. In a joking way they liked to allude to their family legend of foresters; as butchers they had opportunities to make a lot of chopping jokes. At Thanksgiving the year after she graduated high-school their daughter married a man whom nobody knew anything about except for his happy last name. The Coopers told customers who asked about this man the conventional things that in-laws say, and so told nothing, not even what his job was. Two years later when their girl came home—divorced, apparently, though there was a shortage of clarity around that—she was Mrs. Bliss from then on.

"One time my father half lost his thumb in his meat slicer," Mrs. B told the girls. "I was working in the shop that Saturday and when that happened I went running into the middle of Bring Street to get help. But who should come along right then but Doc Weir and Hodge in their car—I thought I was in luck and Doc would come and stitch up my father. I waved like crazy at them but they only thought I was just saying hello. Hodge waved back and they kept right on going up the street. My poor old father nearly died of the blood loss—can you imagine?"

So why is love the way it is? The question worried Juny even before she could put words to it. She was building an idea of love as hungry. The adults who said they *loved* her— her ex-mother, her father, her grandparents—Juny some- times had a picture of them in her mind as crouching wolves hiding in the brush along the Mattabesic, looking for their chance to make a meal of her. It was in the way they hugged her; they squeezed Juny even in the way they looked at her. For years after her mother disappeared Juny felt their eyes watching, the same way Santa Claus was said to watch her in the run-up to Christmas.

Juny never mentioned any of this to her father. He had too many worries as it was.

After Amy Collins disappeared boom times came to Fortunes Neck—new people, more money, expectation, the feeling of abundance. Plans were announced for a connector highway between the Massachusetts Turnpike and Hartford. Then in the spring of 1962 out on Highway 12 in Lordshaven a 300-acre residential development was begun. The site, which the hopeful developer called Eden Hills, included the former Parsons farm.

Eden Hills was the idea of Charles "Pickax" Taylor. He was a wealthy man for as long as anyone could remember, although that wasn't far back. Pickax and his brother Robert came off the farm in the Twenties to start a hardware business. Over the years custom-cut lumber became their moneymaker, especially in the two decades after the war. Home building went through the roof then; that was a joke Pickax always made. He was rich so people laughed, hoping his luck might be contagious.

The other brother, Robert, wanted no part of Eden Hills. "We've got plenty right now," he told Pickax. "Why gamble? Just to get more?" But Pickax was born hungry, as he always said. He was hungry *looking*—thin and jut-jawed; you'd hardly know the big-bellied Robert was his brother.

"I've got the high basic metabolism," Pickax told people whenever he was asked to explain the difference.

It was because he was so thin that the kids called him

"Pickax" growing up—"built like the handle," he would say. He hated the moniker but it was useful to him. In 1954, for instance, he ran as the Republican for Town Supervisor against Bob Trammel, Bring Street's only attorney. To every Rotary Club and voters coffee he carried a pickax to set in front of him when he talked. Taylor was an awful campaigner. He was a self-made man and like so many self-made men he could be tiresome on that subject. His self-creation was the burden of his remarks any time he stood in front of voters. Even in a race for local office people like to hear some rationale for running. It was clear to everyone that Pickax only wanted something new to do.

And he wasn't helped much by his wife LuAnn. Like Pickax she came of a farm background, and she liked having money. LuAnn liked to stress her humble roots but her huge relief at leaving them behind showed through like a secret smile. Even in the way LuAnn said hello she couldn't help sounding like a pretty girl speaking to a plain one.

Anyway, Bob Trammel beat Taylor by a big margin and Pickax was out of the politics business. From then on he folded into his story of self-invention a subplot about the venality of political cronies and the gullibility of voters. It was all about an idea of himself as a maverick. That's how he came to hire Jack Parsons.

The Taylor bothers knew Parsons as a customer going back 15 years to when he had his farm. Pickax remembered him as a friendly but direct young man, a combination of qualities he liked to believe he owned himself. Later, after the fire and the departure of Mrs. Parsons, later Pickax recalled driving past Parsons on Sunday mornings, a lonesome figure pulling apart the wreck of his burned-down house.

"Had that've been me," he told LuAnn, "I know how I would've felt."

Ten years later Pickax heard about it when Parsons lost his job at the radio-fuse factory. He knew it was owing to the shadow that fell over Parsons during the investigation into Amy Collins' disappearance. It suited Taylor's idea of himself as the maverick to hire an outcast, and he would defy anyone to say a word about it. He was also a Christian and was ready to forgiver Parsons whatever it was people were whispering about. Three years later Pickax asked Parsons to be his general manager when he was ready to start the Eden Hills development. Taylor was smart to hire Jack Parsons, who had the multiple talents one notices in farmers.

Still, it must have been sad for Parsons to come to work on the patch of ground where he once tried to make a life. No one had lived there since he gave up trying to be a part-time farmer and sold the property back to the bank that held his mortgage. That was in 1952. By 1959 more people knew Parsons from working for Taylor, although they understood there was something pitiful in his past. It clung to him like the smell of smoke, to make the obvious simile.

So Johnny Collins and Jack Parsons both owed the beginnings of their affluence to Pickax Taylor's talent for prosperity. Johnny often saw Parsons out at the building site. He respected Parsons for his skill. He saw how even the master carpenter listened when Parsons had a point to make. Yet Pickax seemed to be Parsons' only friend in the world. Three years later when Taylor had his next brainstorm—home remodeling—he invited Jack Parsons to be a minority partner.

Now Parsons would have a bit of money too.

Try living in the present and the past erupts around you on every side. The people who later come to live in the Eden Hills development would have no knowledge of the bad luck older residents associated with the place. Seventy houses were going up out there and Collins P&H was contracted to supervise the installation of plumbing in each of them. The day they found the skeleton, in fact, Johnny was super-intending out at the building site. A backhoe was trenching the ground for a powermain when the man tidying behind it noticed the bones fetch up in the dirt.

"Yo, Collins!" someone yelled. "Get over here quick!"

They called to Johnny on instinct, though he had nothing to do with electrical work. As he came forward he saw the other men searching his face for reaction. Then when he saw the bones Johnny guessed what they guessed. Without touching the semi-articulated skeleton Johnny squatted in the turned-over earth and studied it. From what he knew about bones—which was nothing at all—they looked unremarkable.

"It's somebody," Johnny said. "I guess the thing to do is call the cops." He saw at once that the skull was minus a squarish chunk above the right eye socket. On one side of the jaw teeth were broken.

Someone went to the contractor's trailer and phoned the County. Johnny straightened up and went back to work. He showed no awareness of the other men's eyes on his back as he walked away. But he felt them looking.

There was no reason to assume it was Amy that was turned up—what would she have been doing out there in Lordshaven? In his own bones Johnny knew for certain it wasn't her. By then it was settled in his heart that she was gone for good. His neighbors were not so settled, and that's not uncommon in such cases. Even in a modern place a violent departure is never fully forgotten. For people who knew of Amy's disappearance it still gnawed a little. So when the skeleton was unearthed a single thought went around.

A forensic anthropologist pretty quickly established that the skeleton belonged to a man, a man who had been dead at least 500 years. That would have been two centuries before Europeans paddled up the Mattabesic and made a home for themselves at Fortunes Neck; so much of history has nothing to do with us. Something dull—a stick, an ax—took the two-inch piece out of this man's brow; the story of antiquity is of one long bloodbath; just read your Bible. Though no fetishes were found with him the man had probably been buried in the spot where the builders found him; he had not been just left lying on the ground. The funeral urge is a strong one. After all this time it's amazing the world is not a carpet of corpses—how does the ground hold them all?

For six weeks work on the patch of ground where the bones turned up was suspended while archeologists from the University of Massachusetts came and poked in the dirt, looking for still more bones. Nothing else was ever found, nothing—no more bones, no trinkets, no midden, nothing.

Later they straightened the man out and put his bones together with wire. They laid him in a display case set up in the foyer of the Fortunes Neck town hall. He was a proof of history. For 22 years he slept in that glass case collecting dust until lawyers for the Massantuckeet people claimed him and successfully sued Fortunes Neck to have him reburied in holy ground down in Connecticut.

Juny was in second grade that year they found the Indian man. Not until decades later did it occur to her that she hadn't made the connection with her mother's disappearance that the rest of them all did. Not that it wasn't spoken about; it was mentioned in the newspaper, but Juny was seven years old and did not read newspapers. And naturally the adults around her kept it quiet until they knew what was what.

Life went on. In 1961 the Air National Guard built a facility upriver from the base in Windsor Locks. Pickax Taylor, the builder behind the Eden Hills development, won the contract and again he made Johnny Collins the sub for the heating and ventilation work. That meant still more money. Johnny was surprised by affluence. He and Juny bought a yellow Ford Fairlaine, but otherwise they maintained their modest existence on Cottage Row. Johnny couldn't think of anywhere else that he would want to live, and Juny didn't know any better.

Collins P&H outgrew the shop on Bring Street, but Johnny felt no desire for a bigger building (no matter what Miss Most said). He never changed a thing about the shop except for one year when he and Juny painted the outside. Had Amy Collins come back from wherever it was she went she would have found things more or less as she left them, and that was more than three years already.

Even after those three years Amy's essence still float-ed in the corners and behind the doors of the house on Cottage Row in the same way Gramma Jeannine left the smell of perfume and cigarettes behind after she'd been to visit. If she's dead, Juny thought, Mamma should stay away and not make life harder than it already is by lurking in the silences. Amy was always creeping around, especially in the night when—like anybody else—Juny was most prey to her imagination.

Often Juny dreamt of Amy tugging at the sleeve of her pajamas, pulling her up out of sleep. On the edge of bed she would blink her eyes just as she tumbled over, sure of Amy at just the moment when she fell out of bed onto the floor. Sometimes Juny found it funny to fall out of bed and find herself wound in sheets like a mummy on *Chiller Theater*; this often happened. Her dreams made her restless. Half the time she hit the floor with a thump and her father never stirred in his bed across the hall. The other half of the time Juny pretended she was hurt and cried to make him come in and comfort her.

Nothing changes just because we sleep. Dreams were giving Juny intimations of exactly that.

The moon peaked intermittently through a wedge in the clouds. Juny pressed her nose against the cool window screen. Below her moisture hung like cobwebs around the street lamps of Cottage Row. It was a musky summer night, the smells of it vegetable and suggestive. There was a smell hanging on the air out there that was like bread dough. The crickets harmonized, as if all those bugs were beating to a single pulse. Most of the houses were dark now, but across the street there was a nervous blue light in the living room of the Horn's house. Irene's mother was sitting up with the television again.

Juny loved peeking out from her window at night. It tickled her to see the familiar landscape remade in shadow yet remaining itself, only covered in a cream of dark. In summer the natural world goes on day and night, an awe-inspiring thing. The sensation of life proceeding out there in the darkness is company to the sleepless, unless fears get started. But from her bedroom Juny felt safe, knowing her father was sitting up downstairs.

She focused on the radium dial of her bedside clock. The hands pointed straight up, midnight, the no-time, the hour of transition, as Juny understood from watching cartoons. Outside on the front lawn the all-night singing birds in the tulip trees were at it again, as ever.

Juny didn't know it but for a moment she fell asleep with her cheek against that window screen.

She woke when a car went past, pushing its light beams in front of itself and they shined in her eyes. The car stopped for half a minute in front of Mrs. Bliss' house while the driver looked up something in a book. She could see the man's silhouette. There was a woman's voice crooning from the car's radio.

I would be your breath, your blood
The shimmer on a lake
I would be the sun you see
The instant you awake.

What worked on Juny's heart was the idea of music broadcast from a distance, from someplace where people were still awake with the lights on. For her all distances were the same.

A stray dog strolled past on the sidewalk, click-click with his claws on the cement, the image of cool freedom. From inside Mrs. B's house next door Casey began barking. Mosquitoes threw themselves against the summer-screen, hungry for Juny.

Talk floated up from the sunporch right below her. Juny pressed her ear to the screen to see what she could make out. Who owned that voice that was not her father's?

Juny pictured herself as a silken cat tip-toeing to the top of the stairs; animal metaphors are instinctive with us. The kitchen was at the bottom of the steps and the light was off down there. One step at a time, quiet as she could, she slipped down, listening at each footfall, the wood stair gluey with moisture, sticky to the soles of her bare feet. With each step she made out a little better the words her father was saying. At the bottom she scrunched up and then duck-walked to a hiding place under the kitchen table.

Juny never saw sex before, and as far she remembers this first glimpse of it was more interesting than troubling; there is no latency period. Her father's backside, Lily Meursault's wide hips, necks rolling. Like swans. She was curious to note that Lily and her father appeared to be struggling—Lily to stand up and him to lie down. This eye for paradox is not learned but inborn, though even as she watched Juny had the feeling she was misinterpreting. In the unlight of the porch she saw Lily's bare shoulders and one white knee, her father's bare bottom obscuring the rest of it. Lily looked enormous, and Johnny half-resting on her seemed barely half her size. Somewhere before this Juny had heard the word "naked". She was pretty sure that this was it.

It was not terrifically surprising to have Officer Meursault in Juny's house at an odd hour of the night. After Amy disappeared Lily started being around in the evenings and never broke the habit. If she came to Cottage Row it was always after Juny's bedtime. Juny was aware of that, and she didn't mind. Adult voices and the smell of tobacco smoke floating upstairs were reassuring to her. Sometimes she fell asleep with the idea of Lily Meursault in her head, not sure the next morning if she really had been in the house.

Johnny lay across Lily's hips like a man who has dragged himself ashore, exhausted from the effort. Even forty feet away Juny felt the heat rising off their skins. There under the kitchen table Juny smelled their humid smells.

Lily said, like she was continuing a conversation, Lily said, "There's no trail, you know. There never was a trail."

The rugs in the house were up for summertime and Lily's voice off the hard wood floor came up amplified and sharp. Down to this day the sound of actors projecting their voices off the boards of a stage recovers this moment exactly for Juny.

"The next day I knew that," Johnny answered.

Sitting under the kitchen table in the dark Juny was in no doubt about who they were discussing. But she was too absorbed by the amazing fleshiness of adults to stop for that thought.

"It's no good if you're going to mope," Lily was saying. "What's it doing for the little girl if you pretend her mamma might walk back through the door at any time? This is going on more than three years. Think of the strain on her nerves."

"I do think of it. Lately she's been having these dreams."

"That's exactly what happens."

"Sometimes in her sleep she whimpers. If I get out of bed to check on her she'll be flailing around like what dogs do if they dream about rabbits."

A parent's insights are uncanny. Juny *did* dream of rabbits sometimes. She and Casey might be out in a field running after them. It felt like they could run all day.

"The other morning," Johnny said, sitting up to light a cigarette, naked on the settee, "the other morning she comes running down for breakfast and tells me she was expecting to find Amy at the stove making eggs. She gets so excited that she wakes herself up. Sometimes I have that dream too, and I wake up feeling so bad that I just wish I could die, Amy."

"Lily. My point is, imagine what it's like for the little girl."

"I do. And it kills me. But Juny thinks I know everything there is to know. I can't tell if it's a good idea to change her mind about that or not."

"She needs to think you're the man in charge. You shouldn't let that make you shy or you'll spoil things for her."

When an hour later Lily pulled on her clothes and walked

home Johnny went upstairs to sleep. He was alarmed to notice Juny's bed empty when he passed by her room. Right
away he imagined… He didn't know what he imagined. He
imagined Juny gone to be with Amy. (Not all emotional trig-
gers are acquired in the primary years.) Johnny went flying
back down the steps. The instant he flashed on the kitchen
light he found Juny where she was, under the table, asleep.

"Sleepwalking, baby? Please don't start that again. Your
daddy couldn't take it." Johnny whispered to keep from waking her. Juny pretended to be asleep in his arms as he carried
her back up to bed.

The next morning when Juny's eyes opened she noticed
she was feeling unsettled but could not put her finger on why.
Like dreams evaporating in daylight the source of whatever
it was got farther away from her the more she looked for it.
At breakfast she told her father a story of a lady in a bathing
suit. The lady could fly.

For one purpose or another we take everything on board.

Death is beyond the imaginations of children. Their natural condition needs to be hope. It was still that way for Juny three years after her mother's disappearance. Had she come in from school one afternoon and found mamma sewing at the kitchen table she would have been delighted but not really amazed. It would seem more natural to have her mother there than not.

What Juny didn't know was that for her father it was no different, even though Johnny understood very well that life is not forever. What Juny remembers now is the way her father was always saying to people "Good-bye for now", as if he were reminding himself that every parting is temporary.

In those days Johnny was frequently consulting how-to-do-it books on bringing up children, hoping to find a recipe he could follow for raising Juny; almost anything can be found in books. In the week after their late-night conversation about giving Juny false faith, for instance, Lily brought him a copy of *Dr. Spock Talks With Mothers*. Johnny sat down with the book over several evenings in hopes of learning what to tell his daughter about her mother's permanent absence. Scanning the chapter headings—"How Important is Fresh Air?", "Sweets and the Teeth", "The Father's Role in Discipline", "The Whiner"—Johnny found nothing about how a parent might tell a little girl about death. The closest he came was in a part called "The Memory of Fears". This turned out to be mainly comments on the romantic feelings small boys have for their mothers—that and Dr. Spock's observation that "the child's fear of retribution from his father adds one more to his reasons for being anxious about the safety of his own genital." Not a lot of help.

Life's big questions must never be tackled single-handedly, and one evening Lily was speaking to Johnny along those lines.

"You have to talk it over with someone," Lily told him, pulling herself closer to him. She respected the science of psychology, and in the course of her work she also read a great deal in the literature of police work in Massachusetts. She gave Johnny the name of a criminal psychologist in Worcester, Dr. Gerhard Stein. She remembered Dr. Stein from a lecture on cross-dressing at the police academy ten years before.

The impossible happens every day, though this isn't something we should bank on. This was Stein's operating philosophy, his touchstone. He explained it to Johnny the day they spoke by telephone. He listened closely as Johnny laid out the situation.

"I believe I remember your wife's story, Mr. Collins," said Stein at last. "Three years is a long time, but probably not long enough for everyone there in Fortunes Neck to give up hoping. Am I right?"

"For me, yes. But I'm trying to do the right thing for my little girl. And on my part I have to admit it's all guesswork."

"Everything I do is guesswork, too, Mr. Collins. Don't let me kid you about that. But my guesses I try to make based on what's realism. I won't tell you that your daughter will never see her mother again, but you and I recognize that anyone who's been silent three years is more likely than not to be dead." Hearing the word "dead" Johnny winced. "My own feeling," Stein told him, "is that Chief Meursault is saying that you torture yourself with hope by not putting your wife to rest—whatever that means in this case. And from what you say I gather you're more worried about your daughter on that score than you are for yourself. Am I right?"

"It's like we're teasing her."

"You may be."

"I don't know what else to do."

"Contrary to what many people think we psychiatrists don't hand out solutions to problems. Half the time I can barely figure out my own life, believe me. But consider this, and then I've got to go. Maybe you could hold a ceremony for your wife that would put some of this irresolution to bed."

"A memorial?"

"Call it a remembrance. You don't have to hold it in a graveyard. Plant a tree in a park in her name. Something of that nature. Does Fortunes Neck have a park?"

"Waterhouse Hill."

"Well, there you are." For this good advice Stein never sent Johnny a bill.

Sad tales are far from uncommon, to state the obvious. For the Weirs there was the suicide of Doc's sister Millicent, and then there was Hodge's failure to grow up and find an application for himself. But naturally the biggest thing was what happened to Amy. Johnny—correctly—believed the Weirs held him complicit in her disappearance, as if he'd misplaced her. The roots of this suspicion went deep. From the day Amy brought him home the Weirs did not mute their objection to Johnny; this was before they knew anything about Aunt Margaret, which right there was an odd thing. Johnny was simply not what they had in mind for their daughter.

"My mother was in some ways a harder case than my father," Uncle Hodge told Juny years later. He knew how his niece liked hearing the old stories and sometime he obliged her. "I don't think mother had any idea what a snob she was. I remember once her saying to Amy, 'Where will that one ever take you?' I think mother needed a while before she worked out that Amy didn't want to go anywhere."

Even when Amy was still around Johnny Collins understood that his participation in family meetings was on sufferance of his position as Juny's father. A sense of duty is that painful thing—categorical—and where Juny was concerned Johnny was dutiful and so were the Weirs. And so one Sunday in July, 1961, Johnny had reasons for sitting down with the Weirs to talk something over.

In the kitchen of the house that day Johnny spoke with Doc and Jeannine about putting Amy's spirit to rest. Outside Juny was playing ball with Uncle Hodge in the Weir's sunny backyard. They looked untouched by anything, Juny and her Uncle Hodge. Hodge bought himself a whiffle ball that day and he was showing Juny how to swat it with a badminton racket. Indoors, in the cool house, a conversation jinked forward and back between Johnny Collins and Amy's parents.

Darkness and light in parallel: that's the nature of things.

"Dr. Stein," Johnny was saying, "thinks children listen to whatever we tell them as a fairy tale—not like facts the way we do but more like clues of things. He says in some ways they're smarter than we are that way. To us it's just whatever we happen to be saying, but even without using words we could accidentally be telling Juny a story that's confusing to her. Mentally."

"I understand a bit about psychiatry," Doc replied. He spoke in a flattened tone, his effort at patience obvious. From experience Johnny knew that when his father-in-law made an effort at being mild it meant he was irritated and would progress to frosty.

"What could a forensic psychologist know about pediatric trauma?" said Doc. Where another man might shove with his hands Doc did it with a larger language than he used ordinarily. He was a not a tall man but he was big. "Does this man think the disappearance of her mother will make Juny an ax-murderer in later life? That's so reductive, John. I wish you had come to me first." There was a burning cigarette in Doc's left hand.

"I'm talking to you now. Tell me your opinion."

"My opinion, John," Doc said, leaning half across the small table on his elbows, "my opinion is that children are more resilient than we think. And if you don't mind a bit of philosophy, whether we can describe the process or not Juny is learning important things about navigating this life. We don't *know* ourselves except by struggle, and within limits I'm not sure it's an *un*healthy thing for Juny to be discovering that. Even at her age." Doc rubbed the sore place on his leg.

For the moment he let it go at that.

Nominally Johnny and Juny were at the house this Sunday afternoon to congratulate Hodge, who just that month bought a partnership in the Globetrotter travel agency where he worked. Hodge had been in that job not quite four years, since coming home from his six-month try at the Caribbean medical school and the eight years with the Framingham paper company. Travel agent was a good job for Hodge. People liked him. That summer, urged on and partly financed by his parents, Hodge purchased a piece of the agency from Ann and Robert Street, former high-school classmates of his who before that time hadn't considered having a partner. Hodge felt his life coming into focus. Everyone was pleased for him.

"In my heart," Johnny was saying, "I'll never give up on seeing Amy again, though not on this earth. But we've got to look after Juny, and she needs this case closed." He observed how his police metaphor made Jeannine flinch. Now Johnny felt he had been rude, a sensation which he was often feeling around his in-laws.

Jeannine got up from the kitchen table and looked out through the patio doors at Hodge and Juny playing ball.

"Do you ever wonder if Amy might be, I don't know, *someplace*?" Jeanne was gaunt and her hair had no luster. She was growing old. "I do," she said, answering her own question. "You read about amnesiacs who turn up years later on the other side of the country all the time. Don't you, Doc?"

"Not all the time."

"I used not to believe it but to wish it," said Johnny, though Jeannine had not put her question to him. "Something told me almost from the first day that she was gone. I don't know where, but she's gone. So no, I don't let myself hope anymore."

"If ever we let go of hope we all die." Jeannine replied to Johnny without looking in his face; her response sounded like something she'd read.

She stared out the glass of her patio doors, watching Juny and Hodge play ball. Her interior of woe registered in her face; an interesting constant across cultures is how seldom motherhood is associated with laughter. The role attracts images of sorrow past the point of cliché. A painter might have captured Jeannine Weir as a mid-century matron—cornflower-blue tennis blouse, short graying hair, smoking Doc's cigarettes.

"Stein told me that hope is being in contact with the facts." Johnny was pressing his advantage, and he went to work on Jeannine with his appeal on behalf of Juny's mental health. "Stein is right, in my opinion. By not letting Amy go we're making things tougher for Juny than they already are."

Childhood is the closest we ever come to a time of unmediated feeling. That summer Juny was seven years old and still struggling to get her feet under her, so to speak. She was chubby then for the only time in her life; it was just before she started to shoot up. As a grownup she would be as lean as her mother, though never as frail. The Weir features—the fair complexion, close eyebrows, broad nose—were so strong in her that someone who didn't know better might guess that the man tossing the ball with Juny was her father.

"For the first time I see her as orphaned," said Jeannine as she stood up. By this she meant Juny, unconscious of any possible injury to Johnny. "Allow me to orchestrate the remembrance, John, would you? Let me be the one who buries my girl."

So love wraps us one around the other.

One purpose in commemorating the departed, of course, is the opportunity if affords for revisiting old grievances. If we are attentive this can be a way of learning a little history.

With Amy's remembrance Johnny Collins gave his mother-in-law a free hand, the way she'd asked. Jeannine planned to hold it on Waterhouse Hill, apparently by asserting the Weirs' 300-year-old family connection to the place. The only request Johnny made was that Mrs. Bliss from next door be invited, as well as Lilly Meursault and her mother. Their inclusion ruffled Doc.

"There's nothing to say against the mother," Doc said of the Meursault family, "because I don't know her. But the daughter and the old man didn't exactly crack the case, did they?"

They were sitting in the Weirs dining room and Jeannine was writing names on a yellow pad of paper. On the sideboard they had just acquired was a photograph of Hodge dancing with his mother, a pink-faced little boy in a bow-tie, and a snapshot of a teenage Amy looking wary in a satin party dress. The photograph would have been taken before Amy and Johnny were ever sweethearts.

"You think there was a case to crack, Doc?" Johnny was surprised to find himself feeling argumentative.

"You know what I mean, John. If you ask me, I've always thought of the daughter as less a policeman than a novelty act."

If Doc's shot at Lily was something to do with her midnight visits over to Cottage Row he wasn't saying. Something in the flavor of what he said told Johnny that his objection was not about any of that, nor really about the failed search for Amy. More likely it went back to the night Lily pulled him off the barn at the Parsons place; he still resented his dependence on Lily to tell the story of his heroics that night—his main chance at redemption and he had no hold over it. Every time Doc thought about Lily the sore place on his leg throbbed. By this time he'd half lost track of why he resented the Meursaults, just that he did.

What caught Johnny by surprise were Jeannine's feelings about Mrs. Bliss. When he mentioned her name Jeannine's face showed a shock so broad it looked pretended.

"Why *her*?" she asked.

"She's been our neighbor," Johnny said, "and Juny is fond of her."

"Amy never had anything to do with her that I recall," Jeannine replied.

"She only made Amy a little shy," Johnny answered, although he was struck by the truth of what Jeannine said. He stammered as he tried to think about this and speak at the same time. "Maybe it was because Amy was younger compared to her. Didn't Mrs. B used to be one of Hodge's girlfriends? I remember Amy saying that."

"I would hardly say girlfriend. She may have had a crush on Hodge that summer they graduated high school, but that was never any of Hodge's doing. I do recall she never had time for Amy whenever Hodge brought his friends around here."

"All I know," Doc put in, "was that for a while she was around this house all the time. To tell the truth I worried that those eyes of hers might put a spell on Hodge. Boys that age are such idiots."

"What's with her eyes?" Johnny asked.

"Do you remember," said Jeannine, "remember that day Amy made the funny wisecrack about her family that got the girl mad? Even Hodge had to laugh."

"What was funny about the family?" Johnny asked. "I don't recall anything."

"The father was a butcher," Doc told him. "Remember they had that shop on Bring Street, next to the café?"

"First Time Meats. What about it?"

"And Amy started in making puns about meat and so forth—'what's at *steak* between you and Hodge', nonsense things—but you know how kids being silly can swing out of control and all of a sudden somebody's feelings get hurt. Amy could get the devil in her mouth at times, and she kept on and on the more she saw how it needled the girl. We were sitting under that tree right out there, Jeannine, remember that? Hodge was telling Amy to knock it off and I was just on the point of saying she was going too far when the other one stands up and starts shaking her finger at Amy. 'You'll come to a bad end, you little witch.'"

"Pregnant pause" is a wonderful expression. Jeannine and Doc locked eyes, embarrassed by the sudden melodrama. All the scene needed was the sounding of an organ chord. They had almost been laughing. They were knocked off balance, and Johnny saw his opening.

"Put down Mrs. Bliss for Juny and me. She's good to

Juny, and I'm sure Amy would want her there."

Johnny was sure about that. He remembered now that Amy *had* told him the story of the time when she made Mrs. Bliss cry, back before she was Mrs. Bliss. It bothered Amy that after so much time had gone by apologizing only got more difficult, and having Mrs. B in the house next door just made it all more awkward to bring up. Johnny knew Amy would be glad if Mrs. Bliss was present for the remembrance.

Before leaving he also added Miss Most to the list.

National anthems, cigars at a baby's birth, flowers thrown in with the dead: primitive gestures have staying power. For Jeannine Weir it didn't need a moment's reflecting to imagine a tree-centered marker for Amy at the top of Waterhouse Hill. She picked a red oak, a tree known for being indestructible and growing tall. And as she told Johnny, "New England doesn't need another maple."

For the base of Amy's tree Jeannine sent to a quarry in Vermont to get an unpolished piece of White Mountain granite. She had it carved by the same stonecutter who supplied gravestones to the Arcadia cemetery. The first Sunday in August was picked for the ceremony. Dr. Harris Minor, the pastor of the church where Amy was christened, was invited to come. For afterward Jeannine arranged a catered lunch back at the house on Ploughman Road.

Everywhere near-strangers feel entitled to stretch their necks for a look at the transactions of their neighbors— weddings, funerals and so on. The uninvited watch from the fringes, hanging like loose threads. Enough people in Fortunes Neck knew about the remembrance on Waterhouse Hill that they materialized at one o'clock on a Sunday afternoon along with the invited. Mrs. Mercy, who lived around the corner from the Weirs, was there to watch. Once she'd told Lily Meursault how she thought she'd seen Amy walking down the street, and that was weeks after Amy had disappeared.

"I feel connected to all of this," Mrs. Mercy explained to a neighbor as she waited for things to get started.

Naturally we can't help having our personal circles, and within the perimeter of watchers at Amy's remembrance this circle was small enough for them all to feel self-conscious at being observed by the likes of Mrs. Mercy. They'd come over from the Weir's house on foot, and at the Hill they walked as a group up the new asphalt path to the top. They were not to call themselves "mourners", as Jeannine had told them in the invitations, since Amy was not to be called "dead". With no word to call themselves they were off center.

Still they felt ceremonial. There was about 20 of them—including a few neighbors from Fortunes Neck who had literally beaten the bushes in the days after Amy vanished. There was a man Johnny never met before, Roger Bottle, who stood with the Weirs; Bottle was Doc's partner in practice at the hospital. Miss Most stood beside Johnny; on his other side were Juny and Irene, and Irene's mother Mrs. Horn. Opposite, two-dimensional in the white light of mid-afternoon, was Jeannine's brother Laurence and his wife Laurene. They came down from Burlington and would be driving back that same evening. Laurence was a religious man, a bible reader, and he never missed this sort of thing.

Laurence and his wife stood next to Lily and her sel-dom-seen mother. Mrs. Meursault was a tall woman bending toward sixty-five. "Born before the century," she was always saying. That afternoon she was wearing a kind of party dress of a material Johnny recognized as a dotted Swiss. Two bolts of it were in Amy's workroom at the time she disappeared.

Every ritual needs its convener. Doc was head of the family, but he was never any good with words. There's a value in being laconic (people easily confuse it with sagacity) but it does not move things along. For that they had Dr. Minor. In his clerical collar he added the sanctifying factor, though the Weirs were not a praying family. Minor's job was not to offer prayers but to set up Jeannine. She turned to Dr. Minor and said, "Let's get going."

It was a Technicolor day, and inhumanly hot. The people standing around the little tree were all in green-tinted sun-glasses and straw hats. The little paper Jeannine held in one hand was limp with damp.

"Thank you for being with us on this lovely summer afternoon," Dr. Minor said. "We're here, as I don't have to tell you, to remember Amy—gone from these precincts, but from our hearts? Certainly not. Lend an ear, then, to the reflections of Amy's mother."

The form of the eulogy has evolved to give comfort, and for the non-professional it is a risky thing to violate its norms. That day Jeannine departed from convention in such a heartbroken way that she left her audience stricken.

"What happens when we go from here?" she began. As if expecting an answer Jeannine paused. The faintest breeze went around the top of the bill, whispering the baby leaves on the red-oak sapling.

"Our English word mystery," Jeannine said, "comes from the Greek 'myein', which conveys both the idea of silence and of a face with its eyes and lips closed. To me, what has been hardest in these last two years has been the silence. To say so honestly, it just makes me angry when so many nights, lying in bed beside Doc and of course unable to sleep, I imagine asking Amy, 'Now please, dear, tell me where you've gone.' It appears that I'll be asking that question until my dying day. Until then, in whichever direction I look, I find no rest.

"What happens when we go from here? Perhaps Amy has satisfied herself on that score. She always was the wanderer. I see, for instance, that we have Mrs. Meursault with us today. She might recall some years ago when I telephoned in a panic to report that my six-year-old Amy had toddled off from our backyard. What relief I felt when Chief Meursault brought her home an hour later. He had discovered our Amy down the river watching them set up the fish nets they used to have then. Right down there," Jeannine said, pointing. "You can see the very spot from up here where we are standing now. Funny for a little girl to be interested in such things. She wouldn't tell me what she found so fascinating. I should have known then that she would be a willful child all her life. She was a born keeper of secrets, down to this present moment.

"What happens when we go from here?" Jeannine repeated, digging in to her strophe. "I believe Amy has the answer. But she won't tell it. That's a maddening thing. It is a grudge I now have against the world, against life."

The last century's important poem about the surprise of disappointment was "The Waste Land". Rummaging among her books for something poetic to inscribe on Amy's memorial Jeannine appropriated these lines:

> ...the dead tree gives no shelter, the cricket no
> relief,
> And the dry stone no sound of water.

Not much anyone could add to that. Jeannine simply directed the circle's attention to the words on the stone at her feet. She said, "This, I'm very sorry to tell you, will one day serve as my epitaph as well."

Right down to this minute that snatch of poetry and the remembrance oak are up on top of Waterhouse Hill, years after the mystery of Amy's disappearance was all cleared up.

All of them were feeling sundrunk in the quiet that followed so much hard sorrow. When Jeannine finished speaking she took half a step back and closed her eyes, as if a spell were lifted. Johnny feared she might faint. It was the deadest part of a summer day. Up on that treeless hill the sun beat on their heads.

The seldom-seen Mrs. Meursault leaned toward Lily and whispered, "She certainly took the wind out of me."

Then the Weirs turned and began the walk down the hill toward home, Doc limping more than usual and the others following, including some of the strangers who'd come along just to watch. The new asphalt of the footpath was hot and soft and sucked at the soles of their good shoes. Dr. Minor and Miss Most did not go back to the house, and Mrs. Meursault needed to return home to the police switchboard on Nipmuc Street.

Jeannine was leaning on Doc's arm. She clearly wasn't feeling well. Hodge said, "Come home with me, mother." He had been late arriving and left his car at the bottom of the hill. But his mother was determined to walk and Hodge knew not to press. He offered a ride to Mrs. Bliss instead. She turned down Hodge as well.

By the time the others made it back to the house Hodge already had a glass of bourbon in his hand. His face was looking pinched, like that of a salesman who's been told to smile more.

The remembrance guests took shelter in what shade they found. They snuggled under the shadow of the house in summer chairs, eating a bit and drinking whatever was cold. Their talk was aimless and polite; they were mainly strangers to each other. More than that, Jeannine's grief still rung on the air, sharp like the sound of metal, and the nakedness of her woe made them feel shy. When they got home from the Hill she had immediately gone to lie down in her bedroom.

Juny and Irene played whiffle-ball with Hodge in the sunshiny backyard. Allegedly Irene was playing the outfield but the night before she had stayed up late watching *Bringing Up Baby* with her mother and now she was hobbling around like Katherine Hepburn with a heel missing, singing *I Can't Give You Anything but Love.* Sports bored her.

"Give this one a ride!" said Hodge. He tossed the ball underhanded and Juny swung for all she was worth. Sometimes she hit the ball halfway across the yard and Hodge had to chase it. When they got thirsty and their glasses needed filling they called time out. This was a special day, Juny knew, when her father's rules about what she ate and drank were suspended, and she wanted to take full advantage. She enjoyed so much crème tonic that afternoon that she would be up that night crying with a stomachache.

Johnny made sure to sit with Lily and Mrs. Bliss. He was wearing his one blue suit with its knife-sharp lapels. Irene told him he looked like Peter Lawford. He didn't. It was just the suit.

"I think Amy would have been pleased about this afternoon," Johnny said, although this was not true. Amy squirmed if ever she was the center of attention.

"Did she like that particular spot on the Hill?" asked Mrs. B.

"I don't recall specifically that she was ever up there much. It was Jeannine's choice because of the family associations."

Lilly was wearing a swingy cotton skirt and a sleeveless blouse that showed off her strong bare arms. The suggestion of her fleshiness was relaxing to Johnny; he had nothing else to relax him, since he was never much of a drinker, unlike Peter Lawford. Doc was mixing drinks for everybody, glad to have something else with which to occupy himself besides rehashing what they'd only just been doing.

He came outside to join his guests. "How is Jeannine?" Johnny asked him.

"Nauseous. I don't think it's really anything, just her mind spinning around with everything that's in it today."

One good reason for drinking has always been the pursuit

of transfiguration. The big thing is the moment of crossing over; Hodge Weir loved exactly that flash in a glass of bourbon. He was not a big drinker by reputation and he seldom drank alone. But he was a lonesome man who discovered compassion for himself when he'd had a couple. That feeling lasted only a little while; the choice then was whether or not to chase after it; people who don't drink can't know anything about it. That includes children, although the idea of drunkenness tickles their imagination. To them it's magical: pour a little something down your throat and the next thing you know you're reeling and saying funny things in a rubbery voice. Although in Uncle Hodge this was not so noticeable to Juny, who liked her uncle's way of chewing his words even when he wasn't drinking.

More of a puzzle to children is that adults are so often changeable in their moods. For no evident reason Uncle Hodge told the girls that their ballgame was over.

"You hang on to my ball, Juny," he said, flipping it in her direction. Then without goodbye to anyone at all Hodge went out in the street and started his car. For something to do Juny and Irene followed and watched. Mrs. Mercy who had been at the remembrance was out in the street walking her dog in front of the Weirs' house. The dog was Mrs. Mercy's cover for observing the gathering in the Weir's backyard. Lily would later describe Mrs. Mercy as "nosing around."

Uncle Hodge put his car in gear and shot out from the curb. Almost anything can serve to glue a moment in place— a smell, a color, a sound. Even today the flatness of sound on a heavy summer afternoon reminds Juny of the short noise Mrs. Mercy made when Hodge ran into her—*ooo*—like someone caught off guard by delight. When she went down Mrs. Mercy struck the curb face-first. Then her dog was barking and Lilly Meursault was running past the girls.

"Stay right there, Janey."

"Juny."

Johnny was straight behind Lily. The girls hurried after to see what the excitement was. Uncle Hodge was kneeling over Mrs. Mercy and he was shouting, "Dad! Help us!"

The little dog nipped at Lilly and she kicked it in the ribs. The dog tumbled three times before he found his feet. He went off by himself a little way to lie down.

By then all of them were out in the road. Doc was out of breath as he knelt over Mrs. Mercy. "Let's see what we got," he said.

Roger Bottle helped Doc turn Mrs. Mercy over. Her eyes were staring and the face was pale. Around the mouth was blood because her teeth were broken. Doc handled the fingers and the nailbeds were blue already.

"Call up Pequot, Roger. Explain what we have her, but I think we'll let them pronounce."

Lily spoke quietly to Hodge and explained that he should come into the house with her. Before he went along Hodge folded his suit jacket and covered Mrs. Mercy's face with it. She was gone and there was no bringing her back.

The circle that had come from the remembrance attended wordlessly and waited for an ambulance to come. Death stops the clock, and this was a day of death.

What is justice? For killing Mrs. Mercy they gave Hodge Weir four years in Gardner State Prison. Ultimately it would work out that he was released eighteen months early in 1964. Hodge could have done with more time; prison steadied him. In jail grief was the only thing nagging his thoughts. In there Hodge lost himself in meditation on Mrs. Mercy's wide eyes and the sound of her dog barking. The sorrow was so pure it quieted his soul. Hodge wished to pay and pay and pay.

On the day of his surrender the family enlisted Johnny to drive Hodge to Worcester. Doc and Jeannine could not bring themselves to hand Hodge over. Outside the processing room Johnny was told by a cop that he could go no further and must say his farewells.

"Good-bye for now, Hodge," said Johnny. Even as they shook hands Johnny saw that behind his eyes Hodge had already departed for good.

It was around the time of Hodge's "proceeding," as they called it, that Doc first start feeling unwell. All his life Doc enjoyed a good digestion, but in October he was complaining for the first time of a terrible suffering in his gut. On the first visiting day at the penitentiary he felt too sick to make the drive to Worcester with Jeannine. Logically, he attributed it to the stress. He stayed alone in the house waiting for Jeannine to get home, but by midday he was bent over from a pain in his middle so bad he could stand it no longer. He did not even feel well enough to drive himself to Pequot. Doc telephoned Collins P&H and luckily, said Miss Most, the boss had just walked in.

"You sound like you're drowning," Johnny told Doc.

"More like snakes biting me," Doc said.

Johnny told Miss Most to cancel his jobs for that afternoon. He drove over to the house on Ploughman Road and when he got there found Doc waiting on the front steps, sitting doubled over.

"I telephoned your friend Dr. Bottle," he told Doc. "He told me to bring you in."

"Roger's an obstetrician."

"And I'm a plumber."

"Same thing, sort of."

"Bottle knows better than me what to do, Doc." Johnny settled him in the car.

"Once again, John, you're a main character in one of our small family dramas. I should say thank you."

They found lumps in Doc's colon that had been growing there for who knows how long. Doc cursed himself for not having noticed the symptoms in his own body, for having been too dense to take better care of himself.

"Cancer is a roll of the dice," Roger Bottle told him, hoping to soften Doc's self-reproach. "No one brings it on themselves."

"That's baloney," Doc said angrily. "Nothing just comes

out of nowhere." Doc was far from content with the idea of dying. It had taken him by surprise and left him no time to work up a philosophy.

We are all perceptive in our different ways; it's hard to think of anyone who'd say they're not. All through that autumn, for instance, Johnny was noticing how Lily found ways of bringing up Thanksgiving. She mentioned the Mayflower and pumpkins and what did his little girl like special for the holiday? Lily had a harvest-time look in her eye. After several weeks of it Johnny finally said, "Come on out with it, cop."

"I hoped you'd ask my mother and me to cook Thanksgiving dinner for you."

"You cook?"

"My mother cooks. How do you think we eat? On Thanksgiving I cut the turnips."

"Sounds good, Lily. But Jeannine hopes to have Doc home from the hospital."

"She's dreaming."

"I think so too, but I promised to make a turkey." This was the first time Johnny had ever felt the power to hurt Lily's feelings. It annoyed him.

"I have things I owe my in-laws," he told Lily. "Feeling that way makes me still feel close to Amy."

"I just thought you might like dinner." Lily said nothing else about it, but the exchange left Johnny feeling mean.

Doc was in the hospital for five weeks and dying by the minute, but Roger Bottle pulled some strings and got an ambulance to ride him home for Thanksgiving. Johnny and Juny made the turkey and brought it over to the house on Ploughman Road. The two of them cooked all morning. Regard yourself from three steps back and it's startling how obedient we are to custom.

"We never tried a turkey before," Johnny told Juny, "but how hard can it be?"

"Do you want me to read the Fanny Farmer, Dad?"

The Weir's home was a house full of straight lines in the style of that era of decoration. The dining room was powder blue. At the north end of the table, his old place, Doc sat in a wheelchair. He wore a toupee to hide the way he'd gone bald from chemotherapy, and he stank of spirit gum. To give himself something to clutch he hugged a pillow across his midsection. By then he only took nourishment intravenously, though for old times' sake Johnny was in the kitchen making all the Pilgrim foods—turkey, potatoes, cranberries, beets. Johnny had a taste for root vegetables, which he liked for their hardness and lack of affectation. But the aromas of cooking coming from the kitchen nauseated Doc and finally made him wretch. He was sick into his lap and Juny was frightened.

"It's not the cancer that's killing me," Doc said to Jeannine as she cleaned him up. "It's the indignity."

A skill most grownups have learned is knowing when it's time to leave. Johnny and Juny stayed with Jeannine until the ambulance came for Doc and brought him back to Pequot. Before going Johnny asked Jeannine if he could do anything for her.

"What a question," she replied.

Without ever sitting down Johnny and Juny packed up the meal and ate their Thanksgiving dinner in their own house on Cottage Row. Juny fell asleep at the kitchen table while her father was cutting the mince pie. He carried her up to bed. That was hours ago, and now Lily was there.

"Jeannine talks more to me now than she ever did," Johnny was observing to Lily. "She doesn't have the energy to be against me anymore." The air was close with the after-scent of wood smoke from the cold fire in the grate. Outside it was November and Lily's bare shoulders were prickled with goose bumps; it was icy there on the porch.

"She's worried about Doc?"

"She doesn't talk about Doc, or not much. And Hodge, it's like she forgot the poor guy's name. Sometimes she talks about Amy. I guess I serve a purpose."

"What purpose? Why does she talk about your wife?"

"Because she loved her. The other night in the hospital while they were washing Doc we went for coffee, and I'm telling you, Lily, it broke your heart listening to her. She said her marriage with Doc has been a mean joke."

"Who does she think is laughing?"

"I don't know. God."

"Mrs. Weir doesn't believe in all that. I can tell."

"Life would feel more logical for her if she did. If she imagined a higher system with a motive, I mean. Even if it was all made up she'd still feel better. Otherwise she's left with the idea that one thing just leads to another. She can't take it."

When she came over that evening Lily was wearing a beret. Johnny liked that hat on her so much that he asked her to keep it on. She was naked but for that as they conversed. They were snug under a scratchy horse blanket and were smoking in the dark.

"I don't think she was meaning just Doc being sick. She meant Amy and Hodge, and that business years ago with Doc's sister. She was in that frame of mind where you feel like all the things that ever happened to you add up to something pretty worthless. I tell her it gets her down being at the hospital all the time, but she won't listen to me."

"It gets anybody down. To tell you the truth we were happy that my father just dropped dead at home when he did so we didn't have to go through any of that. My suspicion is that he was happy about it too."

"I never see anybody from the staff come by just to talk with Doc. If someone goes in the room to fix him up they look away from him. Jeannine sees how Doc is so friendless at the hospital, even after working there all this time. I asked Mrs. Horn across the street to pop in on him once in a while and she did, but I think she's stopped. They still hold what happened to the sister against him. The younger ones who never heard that story just know they're supposed to be cold to him, even if they don't know why. Nobody deserves that."

"Doc put his money on the wrong numbers."

"Don't talk mysterious, Lily. You make it tough for me to follow a conversation."

"I'm having a conversation too. Maybe you've lived alone without adult company for too long. You've forgotten about the give and take."

Johnny took a breath and said directly, "When you drop hints I don't know what to make of it. I don't have any talent for guessing."

"My father," Lily told him, "liked to use that expression—'putting your money on the wrong numbers'. I know a lot of people thought he was a numbskull but he was intelligent. He just never had a real education. And he could be nice—forgiving, you know? If you're a cop you have insights into human nature, and it can make you more understanding. My father was convinced he was betting the right number. It gave him confidence. When he got my mother and me jobs in the police he thought that he'd done a good thing, that it was happy for our family to be all together. So he may have been wrong, so what? He meant to do right. He believed in God and read the Bible. Even if he was wrong I envied his confidence. I can't personally follow the trail of evidence, but that doesn't mean I don't envy people their believing. I'll bet you Jeannine does too. This is all I'm saying."

"Envy people?"

"Yes."

"If that's how you feel, then who did you give thanks to today?"

"Nobody out in the wild blue yonder, I can tell you that."

The sweat on their bodies had dried and they burrowed into each other in the funkiness of humans naked. Nothing is more primary than lying with your sweetheart in the dark.

"I had no idea you thought about these things."

"They teach you in police school to be indirect. Maybe I've taken it too much to heart. In the end I can't help telling everything I know. Someday it'll be my downfall."

It was quiet, and outside the lawn in front of the house was frosted over. That night there was one part off the moon, and it lay picturesquely on its back. Everyone in Fortunes Neck was sleeping off Thanksgiving. Lying on the couch Lily was more awake than asleep, agreeable to what she had of Johnny Collins. Think of Antiope with her clothes off and you have Lily Meursault in November, 1961; there's no beating those Greeks for archetypes. Her hair flowed around her shoulders like riches. She was different in every aspect from Amy, who had been slight and fair-skinned, and altogether more benign.

Amy was the only woman Johnny had ever been with, before Lily. Not the only woman he'd ever wanted; Johnny could no more be celibate than be a Zulu. But Amy, his high-school girl, was the only woman he'd ever tasted and sniffed and slept beside, before Lily. He would never sleep beside Lily. Sometimes when she was off her shift she insinuated bed in the middle of the day. But just considering the impracticalities of that idea—of Juny and the plumbing business and his interested neighbors—made Johnny so tired that he wondered if something was wrong inside him, if his energy for delight disappeared along with Amy. When he was with Amy he used to feel something fierce in himself, and he missed the way passion once ruled him. Juny was the only thing he was fierce about now, and most of the time Lily couldn't remember Juny's name. He could only offer Lily comfort—the cover of flesh on flesh. Which, by the way, is not nothing.

Lily had him pinned against the arm of the couch with the point of her hip.

"I can boil water for tea," Johnny said. "There's pie there."

"Yes, please."

"Let me up."
She let him up.

In the hospital Doc was in the new wing named for his old boss Arch Cooper. It had the same smells as the old wing—smells of excrement and rubber things—but it was built of clean white brick. Every day when she went into Pequot Hospital to visit her husband Jeannine found that just walking down the sunny corridors evoked her faith in medicine. We trust our institutions because we must.

"The white looks so much less solemn than the old granite," Jeannine remarked one afternoon as she sat beside Doc's bed. "See how it reflects the sun?"

B ack when New England had hard winters the cold was settled in by the first week of December. In 1961-62 it was a deeper winter than usual. Juny had sniffed it coming in October. There was something in the air that autumn faintly like the smell of metal shavings in her father's shop. Juny noticed how in the afternoons the skies were the color of iron and her finger joints ached.

There were early frosts in the Fall and it was a bad year for pumpkins. Even before Halloween that year Juny and Gramma Jeannine had spent two days driving around the Mattabesic valley just to find one good pumpkin that wasn't half rotten. The one they finally got surprised them with a terrible stink when they cut into it, though it made a good jack o'lantern. Juny set it out on the front steps. At night the candle in it illuminated tiny dancing flies. "Pretty," said her father when Juny brought him outside to see.

During this period Johnny Collins was once again paying Mrs. Bliss to mind Juny when she came in from school. Juny was older now and didn't need to be watched over at every moment, though for obvious reasons Johnny struggled with the idea of giving her more room. "I don't want to make her afraid of life," is the way he put it to Lily. Juny was always with Irene anyway, and in their small neighborhood the girls were on a long leash. They only came indoors once the weather turned really cold and the sun went down early.

Each afternoon until she was in seventh grade Juny checked in with Mrs. B and then was free to roam the neighborhood with Irene until suppertime when her father came home.

That winter Juny and Irene went through an interval of intense interest in Mrs. Bliss. Mrs. Bliss owned no television, which in those years marked her as eccentric. And the essences in her house were all different from what the two girls knew. Every home is a cocktail of smells associated with the living that goes on in it. Gramma Jeannine's house, for example, held a cloud of old tobacco smoke, the smell of adults. In Mrs. B's house was the fragrance of decaying paper coming from books stuffed into shelves, the cool smell of a waxy wood floor, the after-odors of cooking and percolated coffee, of steam heat saturating plaster walls, of the dog Casey, who was by that time white-faced and stately.

The secret messages of history are in our senses—coded—and to Juny the smells of Mrs. B's house were not just the scents of adults but hints of *old.* Juny could not imagine how far back things stretched—to a little girl what's the difference between 30 years and 100? By Mrs. B's front door, for example, was a gallery of serigraphs portraying slavery days that Juny regarded as a category of snapshot. A muscled-up Negro man looking full in the face of the sun. A boy sitting outside a cabin strumming a banjo. An old man and a little girl seated on a fallen tree and reading the Bible. A woman walking down a dirt road with a baby on her back.

"Like my menagerie?" Mrs. Bliss asked Juny one day.

"What's that?"

"A potpourri. I like to think that the old man—this fellow reading—that he could be my great, great, great, great grandfather. See what the title says? 'Old pop-pop'."

Before that moment Juny had never noticed how pictures had titles. It made no special impact on Juny that Mrs. Bliss believed she had a blood connection with an African man. Everyone comes from someplace else if you only go back far enough.

"How many years is great-great?" she asked. She'd heard the phrase before but had no idea what it meant.

"Longer back than people have memories, and that's very long. But let's see. My family has been around Fortunes Neck since back when *your* great-great brought men to chop down the trees that used to be on Waterhouse Hill. There's a story in my family that the man who married my old, old Gramma—well, 'married' isn't the word we would use nowadays—anyway, that he was a slave who your ancestor bought in Barbados. He got his freedom when the cutting down was done, and he and his wife built their house on the other side of the river. It used to be called 'the flats' over there before they called it Watermeadow. When I was your age it was still high and dry, and it really used to be flat. It all went underwater when they built the Bring Street bridge twenty years ago. My ancestor sold smoked fish he caught in the river. They weren't smoked when he caught them. These pictures make me think of him."

Juny didn't understand half of what Mrs. Bliss was telling her—she had no idea what smoked fish were—but she found the idea of a deep past amazing; she shivered when she tried to conceive it. The earth and people were not eternal, and still things continued. The beginning of the end for innocence is this first apprehension of paradox.

"I didn't know we had slaves here." A picture took shape in her mind of colored people picking cotton in New England.

"Oh, there were lots of slaves around here. Ask your grandpa Doc about it when he gets better. His people owned slaves way back. When they had no more jobs for them to do the owners couldn't afford to feed them, so they set them all loose."

"Where did they go?"

"That was a problem, from what I've read. There was no work for them, so at first they went everywhere and then they came back."

There are items out there hinting at coherence; apparently in history nothing disappears. As an adult Juny sentimentally associates this with the weak force in physics, but as a little girl she was merely thrilled at uncovering her connection to the hopelessly long-ago. It started a hunch in her that there was something else to know—the thing that enabled adults to go on telling jokes, making meals, Christmas shopping. Most of them didn't seem to be having a bad time.

"When I was a girl like you," Mrs. B was saying, "we told stories about a slave named Stumpy who used to belong to your great-great grandfather Waterhouse. Stumpy ran away one time and tried to go home to Africa. He got all the way down to the docks in New Haven before they caught him, and when they brought him back here one of the Weirs chopped his foot off with an ax so he couldn't take off again. That's how Stumpy got his name, you see. At Halloween we said Stumpy came back up to Waterhouse Hill searching for his foot, but if he got hold of you he'd take *your* foot instead."

The story of Stumpy was less frightening than

disturbing—a new kind of sensation for Juny. For several days she slipped into a silence while she considered not the disquieting story but the idea of disquiet at all. One evening at dinner her father asked, "Why the brown study?"

Juny had no idea what kind of expression "brown study" could be, but she made a guess that it was worrying to her father. She brightened up deliberately, knowing how he needed reassurance.

"I'm just thinking about Christmas," she said.

"What do you hope Santa will bring?" Johnny asked.

In the week before Christmas Juny was at Irene's house making soap stencils on the front windows. They made reindeer and snowflakes and sleighs. Their favorite was the profile of Santa Claus, the hairy old man with fat cheeks and a ho-ho mouth and a jester's cap. Representation is a way of invoking the spirit of a thing.

Jack Parsons was over visiting Mrs. Horn that afternoon. Juny knew who he was. Her grandpa Doc once rescued Mr. Parsons' whole family from a burning house. Mrs. Bliss had told her all about it more than once. At this time Mr. Parsons was still working for Pickax Taylor. That winter Pickax made his big move into the home-remodeling businesses. One of his first customers was Mrs. Horn. She was always saying from the day she moved into that house how Mr. Potts, from whose children she bought the place, how Mr. Potts had left his home in a terrible state. "He must have lived here like a hermit," she was telling Mr. Parsons. The first thing she wanted done was a renovation of the kitchen. Mrs. Horn fancied herself a demon at the stove.

"Are you girls soaping reindeers?" Mr. Parsons. He was standing in the doorway of the kitchen with Mrs. Horn behind him. He was thick around the waist by then and holding a spirit level in his left hand. Juny hated it when adults spoke to her like she was an idiot. Between the two of them Irene was always the more accommodating.

"Uh-huh," said Irene.

"My grandpa Doc is in the hospital," Juny said to Mr. Parsons. She meant nothing by it. She just thought Mr. Parsons might like to know, since they shared a history together.

"Uh-huh," Parsons answered, just in the way Irene had.

Mr. Parsons turned back to the kitchen with his level poised to do some work. Juny heard him saying to Mrs. Horn, "Kids operate on a wavelength they'll never know again when they grow up. I'm in admiration of them for it."

Juny was already in the early days of losing her belief in Santa. Up to that time he was a figure of some anxiety to her, watching all the time, never wholly committed to her name on his good list. The worst of it was Christmas Eve, when the old man sneaked into her room and stood over the bed while she slept, looking down on her, considering her, still not sure what he thought about her. Santa frightened Juny as badly as the idea of Stumpy, and still they expected her to *love* him. The soap stencil she did of the red ghost was the most careful Juny made all afternoon, but on a sudden impulse she pulled out her hankie and witched him away.

"What'd you do that for!" Irene was appalled. But Juny shivered with pleasure.

"I didn't like it," she said. In her mind she was thinking, "I don't even care if he gets mad." To tell the truth it was a relief to let go of the caring.

She'd had one more glimpse of what it must feel like to be grown up.

Everywhere you go nothing persists like clan sentiment. As long as her son Hodge was behind bars Jeannine Weir traveled every Saturday to Gardner State prison in Worchester. She did not tell Hodge that Doc was rapidly dying. For the first three months she evaded his questions about why Doc didn't come with her on visiting day. Jeannine had an advantage there in that something in Hodge told him his father would not come; whatever his mother told him he accepted on its face. Too bad; a furlough to see his father could have been arranged. Already Hodge was establishing himself inside Gardner as a model prisoner. He was in the benign category of gentleman killer.

"Jeannine knows how the story ends the same as Doc," Johnny said to Lily one night out on the porch. It was January. Snow on the ground was old news by then. It thawed and froze and had a sharp crust on top that cut the shins when people stepped through it. The world outdoors was splitting with cold, and the wind bit. Johnny and Lily snuggled deeper into each other under the two wool blankets wrapped around them; the perspiration on their backs was icy. It was a Sunday and they hadn't been together for three days. The previous afternoon Johnny drove Jeannine to Worchester for visiting day with Hodge. He closed Collins P&H for an entire day in order to manage it.

"Until we were talking I had no idea how much in the

dark he was about Doc. I mentioned how Doc seemed sort of low when I saw him in the hospital this week and Jeannine looked at me like I was putting my nose into something that was none of my business."

"Family feeling," Lily told him.

"Why would Jeannine want to hide a thing like this from her son? To me it only seems mean." Johnny was tense with this feeling. He went on talking even as he sensed Lily drifting off to sleep. He shifted her weight off his hip and she stirred.

"Doc doesn't like the son very much," she murmured. "That puts the mother in a bad mood. Between the two of them. It's classic."

"I'm glad you have it figured out. Hodge knows what's going on too. He isn't the brightest guy in the world, but if you grow up in a family like them you develop an ear for things."

Lily rolled over on her back, awakened by the energy of her insight. "The Weirs," she remarked, "always appeared to me a family prone to superstitious feeling."

"What does that have to do with anything?"

"Probably they all associate Doc's cancer with the accident last summer. They blame the son for Doc being so sick. I'll bet even the son feels that way. I'd bet money he does."

"If they do that then they ought to know better. They're educated people."

"People have such thoughts. Time immemorial. We make imaginary connections all the time, even when we know that it's a lot of hoo-ha. Three years ago Doc would have blamed his getting cancer on what happened to your wife. You should thank goodness he didn't get sick back then."

Lily sat up and searched about the sofa cushions for Johnny's cigarettes. She held the blankets around her not for modesty but for warmth. White and naked, Johnny propped himself up on one elbow and watched her. He found Lily beautiful.

"Don't you feel the cold?" she asked him. Her face was strong in the small firelight of the match when she lit a cigarette.

"Not this minute." Johnny took the pack from her and lit one of his own. "Doc and I never liked each other," he admitted, "but on my worst enemy I wouldn't wish what he's got."

Doc waited until the night he died before asking to see Juny; how typical of some people to do the right thing so late that it's wrong. None of them thought to prepare Juny for what she might meet when she saw her grandfather for the first time since Thanksgiving. On the ride over to the hospital she sat in the front seat of the car between her father and Gramma Jeannine. She wore a red-wool coat. A red coat is something no one ever forgets.

Doc was unrecognizable by then. When Juny walked into the room she saw his gown open from behind. He was curled up in bed, half in a ball like something dying in its burrow. On the back of Doc's head the hair was thin and the skullplates showed. He was facing the window and could not roll over to greet them. Clearly he was ripening in a hurry for the other world.

Outdoors the sky was moonless and indigo. The people in the hospital room were all ghosted in the window glass by fluorescent light. Jeannine went around and kissed Doc on the cheek.

"Juny's here, Doc," she whispered. He half raised his eyebrows. "Good," he said.

"Come around and say hello to grandpa, Juny."

Juny kept her red coat on, although Doc's hospital room was overheated and stale smelling. Afterward she heard her father describe the room as "close", and she thought, yes, that's what it was: close. Her grandfather had his false teeth in a glass of water by the bed, and his face was puckered because of that. He showed one bare leg out from under his gown, the one with the ugly scar up high. The skin of that old scar made Juny think of the elastic on underpants.

"Hi, Doc. How are you feeling?"

"Much better, beautiful." Doc reached for her hand. "Your fingers are cold."

"It's freezing outside."

"I love the smell of a cold night. Do you think they'd let me go home with you if I asked?" What is this cultural imperative that demands a jolly outlook on our deathbeds? Since the night Doc passed away Juny has been with half a dozen people at their exits, and all of them tried making jokes.

"How are you liking your school, dear?"

"Fine." She was fascinated to see the transformation in her grandfather; not every shock is traumatizing. Doc was still himself yet bruised all over, wizened like bad fruit; that was the association Juny had afterward in her mind. Doc couldn't make his mouth stay closed.

"What's your best subject in school?"

"I don't have one."

"You must."

"I don't." In fact she was loving arithmetic that year but she felt some stubborn impulse not to please her grandfather by telling him.

"Are you being good for your dad?"

"I go to Mrs. Bliss in the afternoons." Doc half wrinkled his nose at the name of Mrs. Bliss. The old animosity, the beginnings of which Doc must have forgotten by then, was going with him into the ground.

"Is that my mother?" Juny was pointing at the photograph of Amy on the night table next to Doc's bed. There was also a picture of Doc and Jeannine taken on their wedding day. Gramma Jeannine wore a pointed hat on her head like Robin Hood's.

"I miss her," Doc said, following Juny's eyes. The way he looked into her face worried Juny.

"The poor child is frightened," he moaned.

"Come on, Juny," Jeannine said, tugging at her red-coat sleeve. "We'll let Doc rest."

"Doc," Juny said, "did our family have any slaves?"

"I don't understand you, dear." Doc was startled enough by the question that a little life came back in his eyes.

"Mrs. Bliss said our family used to have its own slaves."

"Did she?" Doc's face moved in a way that suggested amusement or something like that. "My great-great whatsus would have had them. Not long, though."

"Let's go now, Juny."

"Mrs. Bliss said you cut the foot off one of them so he couldn't get away."

"Stumpy?" Doc closed his eyes and managed a chuckle.

"That's probably a fairy story. But then we've always had surgeons in our family."

When Doc smiled Juny caught it too; laughter is infectious. She felt a thrill of something like patriotism to find herself blood relative to an historical fact. Then Roger Bottle came in wearing his long white coat and she was tugged away from the bed by Gramma Jeannine.

"Let Doc go to sleep," her father said. Her last look was of Dr. Bottle squatting by Doc and whispering in his ear. Then they said good-bye for now.

Picking over the past changes absolutely nothing. All the same, in the summer of 1962—the summer after Doc went to his reward—Hodge Weir was brought back to Springfield for a few days. He had served barely nine months of his time. Leaving jail was against Hodge's preferences, but Mrs. Mercy's husband Carmine brought a civil case against him which compelled his appearance in court.

All the guests at Amy's remembrance the previous summer—including Johnny—were subpoenaed by Bob Trammel, Carmine's lawyer. Carmine needed their accounts because he had no account of his own. No one had called him to the scene that day when the accident happened. He was in his house the whole time watching the Red Sox play baseball. Lily Meursault phoned him up from the Weir's kitchen, but she had deliberately waited until after the ambulance had already been and gone. Lily found histrionics irritating and she suspected there might be some when Carmine heard his wife was dead; she knew Carmine slightly. If he was going to act that way she preferred to have him do it at the hospital and not at her crime scene, and she had directed Carmine to drive straight out to Pequot.

"Mr. Mercy is a rationalist," Trammel wrote in his brief for Carmine, a hatchet-faced man. He had already rejected an offer of $25,000 compensation from Hodge's insurance company as inadequate. Mrs. Mercy was three-months pregnant when she was killed and that put the price up. Carmine was under the misimpression that he was dealing with a wealthy family, and that Hodge and his mother were a single economic unit. Bob Trammel should have known better.

"Important tactical blunder," Trammel conceded years later to Juny. (There can't have been hard feelings on the Weir side, since Johnny Collins and Hodge Weir both used Trammel to draw their wills.) Just the same, Hodge admitted every claim against himself and still Carmine wanted to press his advantage. In the non-jury trial at Springfield he was awarded $60,000.

Awarding is one thing, getting is another.

According to his statement filed with the court Hodge had assets of $21,412. That included his car and his house less what he owed on his mortgage, plus about $400 in a checking account and the $7,500 he paid for his partnership in Globetrotter Travel just a year before. (The court ruled the latter a "fictitious asset" because it could not be realized as cash.) Once he was back inside Gardner State Hodge asked his mother Jeannine to hire a liquidator and get what she could for his things, which at that time were all in her basement on Ploughman Road. He netted $5,700 from that and selling his car (a hexed Pontiac now that it had killed Mrs. Mercy). Hodge sent all the money to Carmine. When that was done Hodge wrote a note to Carmine:

> *By now I hope you got the check I instructed Rack &*
> *Sons to send. If you didn't let me know and I will make*
> *sure they do.*
> *I know that no money can make [up] for the harm I*
> *did you. I have to live with it the rest of my days. Every*
> *minute I am in here I think about the accident. If I could*
> *trade my life for her you know I would do it in a minute*
> *and without hesitation. My life is over, and even when I*
> *get on the streets again I will always be in jail.*
> *I don't ask you to forgive me. I hope you will have*
> *good memories of your wife to keep with you forever, be-*
> *cause that way she can always be with you and death will*
> *not be final.*
> *This is all you will hear from me on the subject since*
> *words can not describe my feelings. But I hope you believe*
> *how much I mean everything I say.*
> *Regards,*
> *Hodge Weir*

The following summer Mrs. B's dog Casey went to sleep for the last time on the cool wood floor of his house. Mrs. Bliss found him stretched out there when she came down-stairs one morning. In the afternoon she came across the yards to tell Juny and Johnny that Casey was dead. At first

Mrs. Bliss was just telling the story. Then she started crying. She looked away from them when the tears started to come. Johnny touched her on the arm.

"Casey was a good dog," he said. Juny was curious about what Mrs. Bliss had done with Casey's body, but she knew it was rude to ask.

Some deaths are felt more than others. After Grandpa Doc was dead Juny understood his passing as the end of a thread connected to Mrs. Mercy killed in the road the summer before, as part of a story in which one thing led to another and then a final thing. Doc was an old man, and old men die. Also, he'd been at it for a long time. To Juny her grandfather's dying was impressive and at the same time it was out of reach, like something up in the sky. In other words, everybody else's life continued. Gloomy for some of them—especially Gramma Jeannine, who was around much less now except if Johnny invited her over to Cottage Row.

Like Doc, Casey was elderly when he went. He'd been a puppy when Truman was in the White House. But Casey was Juny's oldest friend; they'd known each other at eye level. So when he died Juny was other than sad, which was different from the way she'd been about Doc. Death had directly visited her, and the knowledge of it darkened her inside. Death was tangible, smooth and dense like a cube made of slate, the color of lead, eyeless. For the first time Juny understood that life stops, really stops.

Time is marked in eccentric ways. Juny Collins can reckon almost to the day the picnic at Watermeadow with Irene Horn and her mother. It was on the Sunday after Casey died. She remembers hoarding her thoughts about Casey all that week and avoiding Irene to the extent that she could. Irene had always found Casey smelly and slow, and somehow shallow. Juny couldn't figure out what else Irene wanted Casey to be. Irene wouldn't feel the same about him dying as Juny did, and for a couple of days she stuck to the house and told Irene she was sick. She did feel sick. Then she asked her father if she could spend the days at Collins P&H with Miss Most. She was "in a blue mood," as she heard her father telling Lily Meursault one night.

The weather that week encouraged this frame of mind. For three days it was raining buckets off and on, and in between times the sky was a solemn gray flannel. Then on the Friday Irene pushed Juny's doorbell and said her mother wanted her to come with them on Sunday for a picnic down at Watermeadow.

"My mother said ask your father too."

That Sunday afternoon a breeze blew ahead of a change in the weather. It dried the ground in the spot where they spread a blanket for their picnic. It was August, high summer, and from all the rain everything green was lush and plump, and the sun toasted it all. The meadow grass grew right over the bluff and into the river. The Mattabesic was running high and the drowned grasses fluttered underwater like fish fins, or in Juny's imagination like a lady's long hair.

Emerson wrote that life was meant to be lived out of doors. For one thing fresh air jumps up the appetites, though that was probably not the point of Emerson's remark. Mrs. Horn had cooked a roast chicken and made German potato salad, and Johnny and Juny brought cold potato soup that they made together the night before. They ate it all but some celery sticks.

Johnny and Mrs. Horn were always promising to do things with the girls, though it never happened. It was always one parent or the other who took them places—to the movies, say, or out on the highway to the frozen-custard stand. Juny had already worked out that this was her father's preference. She wouldn't have put it this way, but she knew Mrs. Horn had her eye on Johnny. She planned on casting him in the role of second husband. Juny sensed that Mrs. Horn's strategy that day of the picnic was to make the girls complicit.

Worse was the suspicion that her father knew all about it. He was not himself that afternoon. He was acting like a man too big for his clothes, and he made too many jokes. It was Mrs. Horn making him that way. She buttered his bread. When she poured him coffee out of her thermos she put sugar in it. Juny knew her father didn't like sugar because sweet things hurt his teeth. Then after lunch was eaten Mrs. Horn told the girls to go and pick brown-eyed Susans they could braid into a crown for Juny's father. The girls put the crown on his head and he pretended to be pleased; Juny always knew when her father was pretending to feel one thing or another. She was aggravated with him for not liking these things better, the way she imagined other fathers did. She wished the two of them were at home, just them, or anywhere.

The girls went wading in the river. Normally at that time of summer the Mattabesic ran so low they could have waded the fifty yards across the mucky bottom to the other bank and barely been damp. But from all the heavy rain that week the river was swollen and the girls were in water up to their knees. It was a pleasure to be barefoot and to feel the cold mud of the riverbottom sucking at their toes. Juny liked the sound of that word: "riverbottom". She turned it over in her head as she half watched her father lying on his back up on the riverbank with Mrs. Horn. Only the picked-over carcass of the chicken separated him from her. Mrs. Horn was speaking to him.

"Get enough to eat?"

"Stuffed." The sun whitewashed Johnny's face and made it featureless. His eyes were heavy and he was attracted to the idea of a nap.

"It's good that you enjoyed it. What a big relief to have my kitchen shipshape again and be able to make hot food. For the last two months Irene and I have been eating out of tins like a couple of cats. And I'm the type who feels guilty of criminal neglect if I don't cook my daughter a square meal every…"

"Juny's been bringing home reports about your new kitchen," Johnny said. "Are you happy with the way it turned out?"

"There's still clutter. It was barely usable when we moved in—floorboards rotten, mold under the sink, paint flaking from the ceiling all over things. Say, what sort of character was Mr. Potts? I only met the son when I bought the house, and *he* was a cold fish. Was the old man a recluse? The place had a grudgey feeling when we moved in that I imagine houses have that were lived in by a recluse."

"I think Potts lost interest in things when his wife died. They were one of those couples that was married forever, you know?"

"That would have to be it," said Mrs. Horn, "because the house showed such lack of attention. But Mr. Parsons told me it has good bones, which is a funny way of putting it but accurate. I feel Irene and I have found a home where we can forget all that went before with that person I married. We can start afresh. I'm so glad the girls are friends." Mrs. Horn leaned back on her elbows and stretched voluptuously in the warm sun. She arched her torso.

"They're inseparable," said Johnny.

"That was the word Mr. Parsons used. He told me they seemed joined by a secret radio signal. I guess that's childhood friendship. Once they grow up they'll never know anything so copasetic. Maybe the first time they fall in love they'll experience something like it. They'll be wrong, of course, but there'll be no telling them that. Still, it was touching to hear Mr. Parsons mention it. If you don't mind some crackpot psychology, I think it was because his own marriage ended the way it did, before he was ready for the bloom to be off the rose, that he's sentimental about emotions. It was funny listening to him talk about his wife—not that I laughed, I don't mean that, but in the afternoons when I came in it was usually just about the time he'd be tidying up for the day, his tools and things. He'd spot the girls out playing in the yard or somewhere and make some pleasant remark. It was always clear that he was leading up to the subject of his wife leaving him—can't men say anything directly? I'm sure you disagree, except that you wouldn't for politeness sake. That's what I'm talking about."

"Except to say hello I don't really know Jack Parsons."

Irene's mother scrunched close to Johnny on the blanket, lifting the remains of the chicken out of her way. If one needs to say something one will find an opening.

"Yes," she said, "yes," in a confiding voice, which was the voice she had. "Yes, a friend at the hospital told me the story of how Dr. Weir rescued the family from a fire years ago. Once you start getting to know Mr. Parsons it's one of the first things you hear about. He comes *this close* himself to saying it straight out. For the longest while it puzzled me why Mr. Parsons should bear the Weir family such an ill will. I liked Dr. Weir. Naturally I didn't know him in the serenity of his family the way you did, and of course at times he could act so crabby you'd think he was one of the surgeons. But for all I could see he was a good-enough doctor, though in the course of a day we barely interacted. I think he was dimly aware that I was your neighbor and had to be acknowledged. Somewhere back in the past—before me—it was just agreed upon among the nurses that Dr. Weir preferred being left alone. I heard what happened to the sister. Hospitals are the crossroads of a community, and you hear everything about everybody."

"I guess Doc knew that this is a small world," Johnny told her, "and how stories get passed around." Feeling defensive on Doc's behalf was a new sensation for him.

"My theory, if you want to hear it, is that Mr. Parsons feels like the lesser man because of needing to be rescued, because of the embarrassment of it. It must be so difficult being a man. Or don't you find? Although to hear Mr. Parsons tell it his ex-wife held the same opinion. She certainly sounds like a piece of work. Although maybe she had her reasons."

"When it comes to people's romantic relations," Johnny told her, "never believe a single word anyone tells you." He was making a joke. He wished Mrs. Horn would find another subject.

From downriver came the sound of a perfectly tuned motorcycle shifting gear as it went uphill on Bring Street Bridge. That was Lily flying past.

"Hardly anything is beyond belief," said Mrs. Horn, apparently in agreement. "Not that he told me much about his wife but enough to form an impression. He told me how the day she married again was the worst thing that ever happened to him. I know something about that, you bet I do, and in fact I even offered my own story as some comfort. And besides he's off the hook now for the alimony. Maybe having a couple of dollars in his pocket at the end of a month will get her off his mind, poor soul. I have to ask you this: Is Mr. Parsons a communist? If you don't want to answer you don't have to."

"Is he what?"

"Communist."

"I only know him as a carpenter."

"What I got from another nurse at Pequot was that Mr. Parsons was fired from his job at a defense plant several years ago for being a security risk of some sort. I don't even know what that means but what I heard was that Pickax Taylor was somehow against the government and that he gave Mr. Parsons a job out of spite."

"I wouldn't think so. Pickax was a pretty active Republican. I'm not sure but I'd bet he still is. For some reason he likes politics."

"Maybe Taylor has a gripe nobody knows about. There's still a lot I don't know."

Standing in the river Juny was watching Mrs. Horn prowl closer to her father on the blanket. She didn't like it. Juny had a feeling like jealousy, or like abandonment, which may be a distinction without a difference. She stared at her father hoping brainwaves would make him look in her direction. She wished he would come down the hill and stand with her in the river. He would enjoy how cold the water was.

"Do you think they could get married?" asked Irene.

"Who?"

"Them." Without looking Irene was pointing up the hill toward Johnny and her mother. Her attention was more engaged by blood floating in a stringy clot on the water. She had sliced the fat part of her big toe on a broken bottle and it was bleeding lavishly.

"No," said Juny. She felt actually frightened at the idea of her father married to Irene's mother.

"They could."

"They're too old. And they've already been married."

"People get married again. I think my mother wants to. If

they got married we could share a room."

Juny knew Irene was waiting for her cue to do an improvisation—on *Little Women*, say, starring the pair of them and
Irene taking the role of Jo. But Juny wouldn't play. She was
moping, and in mopery is churlishness. Merging families
with Irene was something Juny felt she was supposed to want,
only she didn't. She pictured Irene and her mother bossing
everything. And whose house would they live in? Juny admired Irene's new kitchen—Mr. Parsons built a breakfast
nook with pink benches, the first she'd ever seen—but she
never wanted to leave her own house. Juny's house was soup-
smelling, the way she imagined her mother smelled. Irene for
a sister would be a pain; Juny knew that in advance. Times
when they slept over each other's house Irene always wanted
to stay up late watching some movie, and then when they
went to bed she lay awake talking it over. Juny liked going
to bed early—not sleeping but eavesdropping. She liked to
listen to her father walking around and sitting down, rinsing
dinner dishes and putting them in a rack to dry, opening the
porch door when Officer Meursault came in. Juny liked her
privacy, and she never minded about Lily. Lily wanted a different part of her father than she did, and a different part of
the day. Mrs. Horn would want it all. The week before when
Juny had dinner at Irene's in the new kitchen Mrs. Horn sat
across from the girls eating pork cutlets and applesauce. She
cut the meat and ate, cut the meat and ate. She made Juny
think of Casey, if Casey had ever learned to use a knife and
fork. Juny never saw anyone be so hungry. Her father and her
grandparents seemed hardly interested in food at all. Meals
were the thing they did before cigarettes. Now when Juny

looked out late across the street and saw the shaky blue light of TV in Irene's house she imagined Mrs. Horn sitting with a bowl or a plate in her lap, eating.

"At least he was faithful to the wife."

"Doc? Of course," said Johnny.

"I'm back to Mr. Parsons. I was thinking of that phrase 'carry a torch,' and what a bad joke it must be for a man who thinks his wife left him because he let his house burn down. Assuming he thinks that. Maybe it's only me who has such thoughts. But I admire a man who keeps his wedding vows. Because I'm telling you, sometimes it seems people went into medicine just to have a bacchanal. The conversations you hear in the coffee room are hair-curling, and as to what I'll leave to your imagination. There's a saying in hospitals that the doctors get younger every year. Lately I'm noticing that the ones who flirt with nurses get older. They're all older. Or perhaps I'm more likely to get flirted with because of being more known as a divorcée. When I started at Pequot there was one representative from a drug company who I swear literally pursued me across the parking field to my car whenever he was in town. He was harmless but he sort of used to lie in wait. 'My name is Buddy,'" said Mrs. Horn, comically lowering her voice to a man's baritone. "Can you imagine a grown man carrying a name like that? I'd be self-conscious. Not him. Nothing could make that man self-conscious. He comes sniffing around every white uniform at Pequot. And a big gold wedding band right there on his finger. He didn't care."

Mrs. Horn wagged her head. Fifty yards away a pair of teenagers kissed. In the late summer sunshine everything smelled like straw. Johnny rolled up onto his elbows and he stretched. Life could be good.

"Irene has a good influence on Juny."

"They're like a pair of wading birds, standing in the water like that."

"Sometimes when I hear Juny with Irene I realize how unfamiliar her laugh is," Johnny said. "She's sure a serious little kid. I hope I haven't made her that way."

"I guess," said Mrs. Horn so sincerely that Johnny thought she was teasing him, "I guess you've had to be both father and mother to Juny."

"I would never try to be Juny's mother. I wouldn't know how, and I'd never be sure if I was doing it right. I know it's different from being a father but I couldn't tell you how. My only worry on that score is how I'll do when she starts asking questions about being a girl in a few years. I hope she'll never feel uncomfortable asking about that sort of thing."

"Men are so sweet when they try to talk about 'that sort of thing,' for all they seem to bluster about it among themselves."

Johnny smiled.

"I'm sure parents find it awkward in general," he said. "Juny's grandmother would help out, I'm sure she would, but I don't want Juny confused about who's running things at our house. I've read how that's not any good for kids."

A breeze stepped up and clouds creamed up overhead; it's in the nature of the sky to shift. All at once the girls were chilly. They splashed their way out of the river and up the hill to their parents. Irene hopped because of cutting her toe. She made the most of it, pretending to be a peg-legged pirate and singing "Yo-ho-ho!" But when Mrs. Horn saw how deep the cut she was angry and swatted Irene sharply across the bottom. Johnny winced and looked away. Mrs. Horn saw him do it.

C hildhood is a river of distractions; the memory of events erodes almost as they unfold. Almost.

In the spring of 1964, when Hodge Weir was released from prison, Juny barely knew who he was anymore or recalled the way she used to like to play games with him. Coming home to Fortunes Neck Hodge wasn't changed in appearance, except for being thinner, but if you're nine-years-old a thing that happened two and a half years ago may as well have happened in the last century; Juny was a fifth-grader by then and her life was crowded. Sometime in this period she heard the expression "disappeared into the blue," and she got the concept instantly. It might, in fact, have launched what would become her life-long interest in probability.

Already Juny was clarifying a realization that there were going to be things in life she would just have to shut up about. As a result she seldom or maybe never had a thought for her Uncle Hodge after he had been gone away six months. The grownups around her contributed to this forgetfulness. While Hodge was in jail Johnny and Gramma Jeannine conspired never to mention him if Juny was in earshot. As a matter of fact, Hodge was back in Fortunes Neck nearly two weeks and living with Jeannine before Juny heard anything about it.

It had to be rough on Hodge when he first came back. He would have looked out on Ploughman Road every day and seen the exact spot where he killed Mrs. Mercy. When the Streets learned that Hodge was home from jail they phoned to offer him his old job at the Globetrotter travel agency. It was a generous thing to do, since they couldn't have known how their customers would react. But times were good then and people were ready to be expansive. It wasn't only that they had the means to travel; they had the wanderlust and places like Portugal called to them. When they walked in the door of Globetrotter Travel to make their plans Hodge's past didn't matter. If anything, dealing with him leant a worldly glamour to their transactions.

As soon as Hodge was making money again he leased one of the houses that Mrs. Bliss had acquired through her one-time husband out on Highway 12 in Lordshaven. On moving day Johnny volunteered to help Hodge shift his clothing and so forth from Jeannine's basement out to the new place. He brought Juny along. It was time to meet her uncle again.

They drove up in front of the house just as Hodge walked out the door with kitchen things balanced on each shoulder. Ever after Juny would think of her uncle just like that: a man with boxes on his back. We proceed by analogy.

If despair really is the worst sin against God then Hodge Weir was in hell this morning.

In the first six months after moving out to Lordshaven Hodge saw his mother perhaps four or five times; two of those times were in Christmas week and once was Juny's birthday in February. Our feeling for each other sometimes wears out, notwithstanding the protests we make that it won't.

"The attachments have died," Johnny said to Lilly one night.

"No family tie," Lilly agreed. It was one a.m. and they were out on the porch. Lily was grateful to have the weather warming up. She always seemed to mind the cold more than Johnny.

"Jeannine's downhearted on her own account," Johnny said. "She's not a bad woman but she's lost all her nerve now. She misses Doc really bad. And I have a feeling she sees her old age closing in already. She's had a lot of disappointments, I know that."

"In my job," Lilly told him, resting on Johnny's shoulder with a blanket pulled up to her chin, "in my job I see people take awful abuse like I couldn't imagine but they go on about their business. They seem happy, even. Other ones take the ordinary knocks and forever after they wander around without any hope. From a psychology point of view," she added, brightening, "you never know who will be which type. My theory is that people just decide which it's going to be for them, whether they know they've decided or not. They make up a story to tell themselves and then they stick to it. It becomes like their religion."

If Lily was right then Hodge Weir's story in the second half of his life was a steady perfecting of his long recital of dismay. Not that he ever said a word out loud about it.

On some Sundays Johnny and Juny went out to see Hodge at the place he was renting from Mrs. Bliss. Not because Johnny was fond of Hodge; it's hard to say what

Johnny felt for him. As in-laws they would have had a shotgun friendship no matter what. But also Johnny knew Hodge was dispossessed; his soul was a Sahara. At times when Hodge smiled he appeared almost feeble-minded, so distracted was he. It was the effect of an ice-cold inwardness, which in certain moods Johnny thought was a category of self-love; he agreed with what Lily said about the choices people make for themselves.

The travel business was thriving and Hodge was needed six days a week. Outside of that he spoke to no one as far as anybody could tell. Who knows what Hodge would have become if he hadn't been compelled by his business to do even the basic to-and-fro with other humans? Hodge had nothing. No furniture. Nor a car, nor pictures for his wall. Nothing.

"This isn't doing much for your outlook." Johnny was looking around one Sunday at the nakedness of Hodge's digs. "You've got money in your pocket again, man. Use it to brighten things up for yourself."

So Hodge ordered a long low sofa covered in a stippled fabric that Juny liked to press her cheek against. It was raspberry-colored. He bought boxy side chairs and a television hidden in a mock-mahogany cabinet. He sent for three color landscapes of the American southwest, long pictures flatly lit. He bought a blue Impala automobile that had straight lines like a tabletop. There he stopped.

"He lives all alone in the whole house," Juny reported to Irene. She knew Irene to be half in love with her uncle, though Irene remembered even less than Juny about the times when Hodge used to come to Cottage Row and play games. Or when he used to wave to them from his window in the office of Globetrotter Travel. Irene just liked the romance of tragedy in Hodge's past. She invented movies that she described to Juny in which Hodge and she lived in the house on Highway 12, sometimes as wife and husband, sometimes as daughter and father, but always as farmers. Juny liked to feed Irene information just to see what came out of her head.

"Would he ever come here?" Irene asked.

"We go there. My father thinks it bothers Uncle Hodge to drive after dark if he doesn't have to."

"Because of what happened?" Irene loved saying that.

"Yes. Last Sunday we took Mrs. Bliss out there for dinner. My father cooked us all sauerbraten. Did you ever have it?"

On the drive out Johnny was always sure to point to the houses going up in Eden Hills as they came over the rise into Lordshaven. People were at that time beginning to refer to Lordshaven as "Eden Hills" after the name that Pickax Taylor gave his housing tract. The second and third phases of the development were going in about then. Taylor's timing looked perfect. That winter the Massachusetts turnpike commission announced final plans for the connector that would bring traffic in a straight line between the Berkshires and Springfield. Its path was right through Fortunes Neck and Lordshaven, and when that happened more people would come in to the area. The swelling density of population was visible almost from day to day, even in the countryside out around where Hodge was living. Juny could remember when the landscape surrounding Fortunes Neck was principally cornfields. Now from the kitchen window of her uncle's house she watched the skeletal beginnings of the homes coming over the hill. On the whole Juny liked progress; she would always be deficient in nostalgia and was very clear-eyed about the movement of history.

Sometimes on the way out to see her uncle Juny's father pulled in among the mud and the cement foundations and the stacks of two-by-fours. Johnny was once again Taylor's subcontractor for the plumbing and heating work, and he told Juny that he liked to make "surprise inspections". She knew he was joking but the phrase made her tingle with anticipation of a glimpse into the clockwork under ordinary things.

For a few months that year Hodge's neighbor next door was Jack Parsons. Mrs. Bliss was renting Parsons the other one of the two houses she owned in Lordshaven. Parsons was between jobs at the time and conserving cash. In July the Taylor brothers had their lumber yard burn down, putting him out of work. Fire had interrupted Parsons—again. For his patron Pickax Taylor the fire was the end of the line. His inventory of lumber was reduced to charcoal. The fire also destroyed a freight truck filled with appliances for the new homes Pickax was building out in Lordshaven—the same houses Juny could see out the window of her uncle's kitchen. It was all insured, naturally, and everyone expected Pickax to start right up again.

"Never mind about that," he said, and said to general surprise. "My run is over. No more for me. That's all I'll say."

It was as if old age had caught Pickax from behind all of a sudden and all at once. His brother Robert, the one who never married, took his insurance settlement and moved to

Arizona, where the air is dry all the time. But Pickax and his wife Norma never lost their taste for bad weather. They stayed in Fortunes Neck the rest of their lives. Pickax held on to a view of himself as the partisan of Jack Parsons, however, and after he made the decision to get out he did Parsons one last favor.

Irv Trammel was the younger brother of Bob Trammel, the lawyer who'd represented Carmine Mercy in his suit against Hodge Weir. Irv was the principal insurance broker in Fortunes Neck and Pickax was among his customers. Parsons, Pickax told him, was the partner that Irv never knew he needed.

"Jack's a good fella," said Pickax. "He learns anything fast. He'd be good at your business—people take him seriously even if they don't take to him directly, if you know what I mean by that. Lord knows he can talk from experience about fire insurance." When Pickax was a boy he read someplace that successful men always seal a deal with a joke. He never forgot this bit of advice.

At the end of that summer Irv agreed to take on Parsons at straight commission. That way Irv had nothing to lose. And just as Pickax predicted Parsons made good—or anyhow moderately good. He never had to look for work again.

From then on Parsons worked out of an office just a few doors down from Hodge Weir's travel agency on Bring Street. But for about five months in 1964 he and Hodge were living sixty feet apart. In all that time they never exchanged a word, not so much as good-morning. Parsons never forgave Doc Weir for rescuing him, and to be consistent he extended the feeling to the Weirs generally. Imagine the concentration it takes to hold a grievance like that for a lifetime. All that energy.

Say what you want about it, money makes a lot of things easier. In those days Johnny Collins pictured himself as a man on whom the world was snowing dollars; in his savings account the cash piled up in drifts. It bought them a new yellow car.

The Eden Hills project was so large it was almost more than Johnny could handle and still keep up the bread-and-butter housecalls of Collins P&H. Almost every day he had to be out in Eden Hills. In the last six months of 1964 Juny ate dinner next door with Mrs. Bliss almost every night. She discovered that her father was a better cook than Mrs. B— by a long shot—even if what he mainly made were soups, casseroles and stews. By then that was Juny's archetype of cuisine. Even as an adult she never learned to like what she thought of as "separated food". Still, Juny was always fond of that period of months when she was spending dinnertimes next door.

That September money snowed on Mrs. Bliss as well when the homebuilders behind Eden Hills—the ones who'd taken it over from Pickax Taylor—offered $45,000 for her land on Highway 12, including both the houses on it. She accepted. Hodge, her old friend from high-school days, moved into her house temporarily, which turned out to be until they carried him out of her house in 1987, dead.

After Uncle Hodge moved in with Mrs. Bliss he came

down the street dependably at six-thirty each evening. Juny kept one eye on the clock, and when she heard her uncle's footsteps on the sidewalk in front of the house she knew it was time to go next door and have her supper. She looked forward to these meals the same way Irene Horn looked forward to a favorite TV show. Most evenings she interrogated Mrs. Bliss and Hodge about all that had happened in the past. Telling about the past—the past before Hodge killed Mrs. Mercy—was about the only time Juny remembers anything like animation in her uncle's manner. Apparently everyone needs to tell their story, whether they know it or not. Sometimes Hodge even laughed when he talked. But then he would notice himself and shut the laugh right down, as if putting joy back in its cage.

"How did Grandma Jeannine meet Doc?"

"You know that story, Juny. She was visiting Uncle Laurence in Boston and broke her wrist ice skating on the Charles. Dad was a new doctor then so they gave him the job of setting broken wrists. Kismet."

"I know. But how did they get from there to being married and moving to Fortunes Neck?"

"For Dad it was always on the cards to come back to Fortunes Neck. This is our family seat. Mother decided he was a live one, I guess, and on the spot she made up some story about having relations in Springfield. Dad asked if he could show her around the next time she was there, or so she says. Mother didn't have family in Springfield at all, but she came down and stayed at a hotel. She picked out somebody's house on a street, gave Dad the address, and waited out front for him to come get her. Ask her sometime and she'll point it out for you. She likes to tell that one."

"It doesn't sound like something she'd do."

"Her brother Laurence was very angry with her for it."

"What kind of things did my mother say?" Though she never went near the story of Mrs. Mercy the subject of Amy was never out of bounds, perhaps because nobody felt implicated by what had happened to her.

"I don't remember things Amy said. She taught me to dance, I remember that. She was a very good dancer. She knew all the steps."

"But what sort of things did she say?"

"I honestly don't remember, dear."

"She had a sharp tongue at times," Mrs. Bliss put in. "She took after your uncle." Juny perceived this correctly as some sort of jab at Uncle Hodge from Mrs. B, but she didn't know what it might be about. Hodge pretended Mrs. B was only teasing.

"Was she funny?" Juny asked.

"Telling jokes and things?" Uncle Hodge tried to think about that. "The same as most people," he said. "She could be a wise guy, she had that kind of humor. Not everyone liked it. But I don't think she was ever mean, or meant to be mean. Maybe once or twice. When she was your age she could make us laugh at the dinner table. Our family used to have dinner together every night, no excuses, not even from my father. After Amy met your father she got serious quick. I remember how that impressed me. I didn't think people could make themselves over so fast as that. Amy really wanted to get on with things. She changed herself overnight into a woman."

"How come Mr. Parsons doesn't like our family? Doc

saved his life."

"I wouldn't say he doesn't like us, Juny. For some people it's hard to say thank you, that's all it is, I think. It embarrasses them, so they act funny about it. Tell you the truth, I don't know what his story is. You'd think if someone ever got a second chance at life they'd make the most of it and be glad. Parsons doesn't seem to, I don't know why."

"It might be that he can't forgive himself for needing help," said Mrs. Bliss. Juny's ears twitched. This was another jab.

If ever Mrs. B challenged him for an error of fact Uncle Hodge smiled and was silent. It appeared to wear him out anyway, talking. Irene was the one who pointed this out to Juny. Irene took this for the good-natured acquiescence of a rogue-male broken at last. She found it terrifically romantic that Juny's uncle was finally together with Mrs. Bliss. At night, she told Juny, at night she looked across the street from her bedroom window and saw lights on in their house. She imagined Hodge and Mrs. B sitting up in chairs, retelling the legends all night long.

Assuming you have an ear for it there is portentous music playing on the air all day long. In the spring months of 1965 it was in the noise of the connector being laid down across the Mattabesic River. Bulldozers shifting and scraping, the intermittent thud of dynamite cracking bedrock, the thrill of jackhammers. Almost every afternoon after school Juny and Irene joined a parade of kids over Bring Street Bridge to watch the work. In October the highway would come out of the trees on the other side of the Mattabesic—it was going to cross upriver into Fortunes Neck and then keep going all the way to Springfield—but already by March the bridge supports for the highway were up and waiting.

On the wall of her office on Nipmuc Street Lily Meursault plotted the path of the highway on a streetmap tacked to the wall. The route went across the middle of Watermeadow and around the north side of Waterhouse Hill. On the south side it made an oval with the bend in the Mattabesic. Inside the oval was the Bring Street business district, including Collins P&H—"the charmed circle," Lily called it. Rents and property prices crept up. There was a fat feeling of money coming, in the back of the teeth a feint electrical tingle, and a lot of people felt their capitalist muscles twitch.

On a sunshining Friday morning in May that year Johnny Collins had a visit from Bob Trammel, the attorney.

"We're shopping a price for sandblasting the buildings

on this end of Bring Street," Trammel told Johnny. He had his office three doors down from Collins P&H and almost directly across the street from Globetrotter Travel. "May we count you in?" he asked.

"Who is 'we' in this case, Bob?"

"The other ones I've canvassed."

A pretty phrase in English is "stretch the truth", which Johnny suspected Trammel of doing in claiming the renovation of Bring Street was a grassroots movement among the merchants. But that's how things are made to happen. And Johnny recognized that his premises could do with a face-lift. Before he had it the building was a Firestone store run by Edgar Portman. After Portman died in 1953 Johnny and Amy took a deep breath and borrowed money to buy the building and move Collins P&H from the basement Johnny was renting at that time. Miss Most like to remind him from time to time that the exterior hadn't been cleaned since the Hoover administration. He only thought to wash the windows three or four times a year, and then only when Miss Most suggested it. Between the cornices the sheetmetal sign that read

Collins Plumbing & Heating
OR6-1830

bled rust.

Though no one would call him cheap Johnny was a careful man with a dollar; thrift is a virtue. He agreed to go in with Trammell to have the buildings sandblasted. Once that was done he elected to paint the place himself.

Decades after we forget everything else our animal nature recalls the weather of a particular day. Rain poured the night before Johnny planned to paint, and it kept up until just before sunrise. When the sun came up a new breeze blew out of the northwest and by eight a.m. the air was so fresh, so kiln-dry, that breathing made the lungs ache slightly. This was a day when the beauty of the observable world impressed itself. In the new sunlight the stripped old brick of Collins P&H resembled pottery biscuit. The facade looked oddly embarrassed. It was a perfect day for painting.

"It's like it's smiling," Juny said when he and Juny pulled up that morning. Her father joked that the building looked like a hobo that got himself a haircut and a bath.

They had tied a ladder to the roof of their yellow car. In the trunk were fourteen gallons of white paint. Johnny promised his daughter five dollars if she helped, and Juny loved the idea of getting paid; in our culture the primary stage of our self-conception is completed the first time we receive a price for our labor. Juny had a new hogs-bristle brush and her father showed her how to paint bricks with it, side to side. People passing stopped to ask how things were going and compliment Juny on her obvious talent. The river down the hill below Bring Street mumbled distractedly and birds sang all morning, making Juny think of bells. Once she looked across the street and saw her Uncle Hodge looking toward her through the window of his travel agency. She waved to him and Uncle Hodge waved back.

Juny was waiting for her father to declare that it was lunch time. She was light-headed with the emptiness in her stomach, a pleasant feeling if there's a promise of a meal in the near future. Officer Meursault came down Bring Street with a carton of coffee from the Café; Juny could smell it.

"That's an admirable piece of work you've done today," Lily called up to Johnny. Lily appeared to be in a very good mood.

"I'm just the helper. Juny's boss on this job."

"Nice work, Janey." Juny played with the thought of Officer Meursault as her father's wife, and that they were a family. She found she didn't mind.

It's all about sex. When Johnny climbed down the ladder Lily said all the nice things about the paint job—why wouldn't she?—and when he answered Juny noticed how Office Meursault watched his throat move up and down, as if that was reminding her that she was hungry too; appetites are other. It was the first time Juny ever felt compassion for an adult. Other than that which she sometimes felt for her father.

Lilly walked off with her coffee and Johnny climbed back up on his ladder. In a few minutes he called down to Juny to hand him up a roll of masking tape. She climbed up three steps and when she reached up the tape her feet forgot what they were doing. She fell on her back on the sidewalk; considering our clumsiness it's surprising that most of us are still in one piece. Juny was proud that she didn't cry. But she couldn't get breath enough.

"Calm down, baby," said her father. "You knocked the wind out of yourself." Even lying on her back Juny thought that was a funny way to say it. Although apt.

"Time for lunch," her father said then, and he took her up the street for grilled cheese at the café. Then he paid Juny and gave her the afternoon off.

KEVIN McDERMOTT

Below the shops on Bring Street there used to be a ferry landing. Right up to the First World War the quickest way to move goods to Springfield and Hartford was still the river, and the ground down there had been a bald and busy place. Fifty years later it was overgrown with brush and birch and maples, almost sylvan. There was a narrow trail that the kids followed. It began behind Collins P&H and went up the river through a half mile of scrub all the way beyond Watermeadow. The track followed the floodplain and was packed hard by use.

At the riverside it was possible to sustain an idea of wildness. For a time that year Juny and Irene spent a lot of hours playing in the scrub along the river. Then some boys from their school discovered the spot. The boys skulked in the brush pretending to be jungle fighters. They crept up on the girls and pulled them to the ground, yelling in their face, "Say uncle!" The boys had snotty breath. Now they'd built a fort of scrapwood right by the water. Five dollars in her pocket, Juny didn't see any boys around but still she steered clear of that place as she started out.

The dirt path led upstream under Bring Street Bridge. In the shade down there at the water's edge the air was cold and aromatic with mineral smells. Juny saw a green turtle moving in the weeds at her feet. She stayed awhile under the bridge listening to cars passing overhead. Each one hummed its tires in the instant before ringing the expansion joints. There was a funny sort of no-rhythm to it. She chewed over her father's phrase "break for lunch"; put a separation in what you're doing, arrest time.

Just a month earlier the places where Juny walked would

have been flooded under the river's spring tide. Now the low ground on either bank had resurfaced and Watermeadow was all greened up. It was nearly summer now. The river was no longer at floodtide even after all the rain they had the night before. The Watercourse was running so shallow that Juny could jump across when she came to it. When she landed on the opposite side she nearly stepped on what appeared to be the same green turtle she'd seen under the bridge.

Juny hadn't been down as far as Watermeadow since a picnic with Irene and her mother the year before. In the hot sun the earth in that place smelled cooked. Just there the t-shaped footings of the highway bridge stomped across the Mattabesic. With still no road to hold up they made Juny think of the old Indians lifting their arms to the sky in prayer. By this time weeds and saplings had put down roots around the base of each brace. Nature was shoving back.

Since the bridge supports were put in back in March the fill packed around them had been steadily redirecting the current of the river. Years ago that place used to be called the Flats, but after the Bring Street Bridge was built in the Forties the spot had steadily been submerged. Juny had never known the opposite shoreline when it wasn't a steep hill that ended under water. Now the prow of the opposite bank was being eaten by the altered waterflow. Trees and all were un-dermined and fell into the water, carried off. Where Juny was standing on the opposite bank Watermeadow had put on a compensating extension of ten yards or more. Just a week ago the muddy edge where she was poking with a stick was under three feet of river. Now boulders were beached among spring daisies. There was a broken lobster pot from

God knows where and near that the wings of her mother's shoulders lifting out of the muck.

In the generous heat the mud on Amy's back and in the tangle of her hair was drying to the color of sandblasted brick. There was a whooshing sound in Juny's ears. The mid-day sun was in its mood of summer kindness, when we feel an impulse to turn our face up to it.

At six o'clock Johnny Collins called it a day and drove home. There was the pleasant smell of paint still in his nose and the nice satisfaction of a full-day's work. Driving down Cottage Row the birds sang up and down the street, and in the tulip tree out in front of his house the all-night singing birds ignored him and went on chattering. What a lot of gossips they must be, Johnny used to think.

The sun backed off while Johnny washed his face and had a cigarette. For later that evening they had plans to see a movie with Irene. He shouted hello up the stairs at the back of the kitchen but Juny wasn't home. Only a little worried Johnny went next door to Mrs. B's to see if Juny had gone there for supper. But the house was locked and the car was gone. In his splattered pants Johnny went across the street to Irene's house and rang the bell.

"Hello there, sweetie. Is my Juny here?"

Irene looked out from the interior twilight of her house. "I didn't see her today. My mother took me to Framingham to see my father playing the piano at the bandshell. Is it time to go to the movies?" In the gloom of the room behind her the television screen was half visible. A man with a deep voice spoke over the pictures. A commercial.

"Not for another hour. When Juny's not with you where does she play?"

"Sometimes up the Hill. Or sometimes on the river. A lot of the time we go and watch the highway."

At that moment Hodge and Mrs. Bliss drove down Cottage Row. Mrs. Bliss was in the passenger seat, sitting up stiff and watchful like an auto-school instructor as Hodge held the wheel. Johnny rushed into the street and Hodge braked sharply. On second thought timing only seems like everything.

"Help me find Juny." The sharpness in Johnny's voice startled him. "Irene!" She was watching Mr. Collins from the doorway of her house. "Sweetie, ask your mother can you ride with us around to look for Juny."

"Yeah!" Irene burst from the house, thrilled at the prospect of adventure.

"Tell your mother you're coming with me."

First Irene sent them out to the roadworks. On an early Saturday evening it was quiet and muddy there. The earth-moving equipment lay in heavy sleep. Next they went to Waterhouse Hill and walked up to the spinney where the girls used to play orphan, right beyond Amy's tree. But a thing in the breeze up there satisfied Irene that Juny hadn't come by that day. She took them to the playground at school, but once again it felt to Irene that no one had been there at all that Saturday. Hodge, who forgot himself in his worry for Juny, suggested going by his mother's house on Ploughman Road.

"It would be a long way for Juny to walk," he said, "but mother may have seen her and picked her up in the car." But when they went there Jeannine's house was in darkness.

"I bet she's at the river," said Irene. She was in the backseat next to Johnny and when she spoke he felt his frame go rigid. Ronald Meursault had said the same thing the night Amy disappeared.

Climbing out of the car in front of Collins P&H they heard the shivery sound of flowing water. In the failing light the building glowed in its new coat of white paint. But no one said a word about the paint job. The birds in the neighboring trees were going to sleep now.

Night rises in clumps. Already it was dark under the trees along both banks of the Mattabesic. But Irene knew the path by heart. She was proud of how she could stride along in the dark as the grownups tried to follow. She pictured herself the heroine in a movie about a lost child. It was Irene leading them over the Watercourse. Irene taking them up to the meadow. Irene shouting out to Juny in the place where she sat. It was the same as dreaming.

It disturbed the adults to imagine Juny alone for such a long time with the corpse. Not only because it was grizzly but because it was tremendous. Death is big.

When they walked up to her Johnny squatted down in front of Juny. With great effort he averted his eyes from Amy's back and looked into his daughter's face.

"It's late," he said. "We should get home, baby."

Without a fuss Juny got up and even thought to dust the
seat of her pants with slaps of her hand. She walked back
along the river edge to Bring Street with them. She said
nothing. All of them said nothing; even Irene picked up that
cue.

That night they asked Irene to sleep over; Mrs. Horn was
prevailed upon to say yes. The girls stayed with Mrs. Bliss
and Hodge while Johnny telephoned Lily. Juny fell asleep
and Hodge carried her up to bed. *Sun Valley Serenade* was
on television, and Mrs. B and Irene stayed up to watch it.
Hodge went out for a walk.

Johnny drove back to the shop again and in full darkness
picked his way down the trail that ran along the river. He
went up again to Watermeadow, finding his way along the
path by the beam of his flashlight. When he made his way
up to the spot where the body was Lily was already waiting.
She was poking in the ground around the body with a spade.

"Hold the beam more steady, please."

The flashlight Lily gave him was big as a truncheon; it
was once used that way by her father. She dug away around
the body the way an archeologist would, chipping at the dirt.
Literally Amy was unearthed. When the body was exposed
Lily tossed the spade aside and worked her hands under the
hips and shoulders. Gently she turned the body over, half
worried that it might break apart unpleasantly. Lily was surprised to find Amy rigid, as if her corpse had been hard-
stuffed with straw.

The body tipped over and for the first time in seven years
Amy Collins was facing up at the sky. Lily was kneeling, and
silent.

"It is," Lily said finally. The eyelids were half open but there was nothing behind them.

They thought it was over.

At numerous points in the hunt for Amy Collins the searchers had been down to Watermeadow. They made good guesses about where she would be, and with clam-diggers' rakes they dragged the river only yards from where the body was lying. But at the water's edge the springtime flooding of 1958 hid the body in just a few feet of muddy water, and it was rapidly buried in silt. Later Juny was the one who remembered the way it rained for days after Amy disappeared, and she had been only four at that time.

"Me and Doc played cards all the time because we couldn't go outside," she reminded them.

Only when the new bridge redirected the water flow eight years later was the corpse on dry land again, in a place where only kids would come.

The body was in excellent condition, like a Viking set to rest in an Irish bog. The skin was tanned and puckered but the face was recognizably a young woman's. The red rayon scarf was still around the throat, though it was mealy with rot. Remembering that scarf was what took Johnny's breath away when Lily rolled her over.

"Funny the things that get you," he told her later.

"Probably she slipped," Lily had concluded immediately. She was pointing at the four-foot boulder next to the head. On the forehead was a black crease where the skull was cracked. "If she fell face-first she must have drowned. Had to."

Half an hour later an ambulance crew came and removed the body to the morgue at Pequot Medical. The next morning an autopsy was done. From the state of the lungs it was difficult to support Lily's theory of death by drowning, though the evidence pointed that way. Anyhow, what did it matter? Knowing wouldn't have changed anything.

"Don't like to hurt your feelings," said the mortician Daniel Pennymaker when he spoke to Johnny in the afternoon. "Don't like to hurt your feelings, Mr. Collins, but the body is beginning to cave in as she dries out. The internment'd better be tomorrow, if you were to ask me. Any funeral you'd better do quick."

Johnny said nothing either way when he learned that Pennymaker had thrown Amy's petrified clothing in the rubbish; there are moments when we don't care if we're in someone else's hands. Pennymaker dressed the body in an off-the-shoulder pink shroud that looked like a nightgown. He allowed Johnny's wish to be the one who closed the lid on the box. No one was in the viewing room when Johnny kissed Amy on the mouth.

The funeral was on a workday. The night before it rained—again—and at daybreak everything was dripping. Before going to her nursing job that morning Mrs. Horn sent Irene across the street in her good dress. Johnny and Juny found Irene waiting on the front steps when they came outside at half past eight to drive to the cemetery in Lordshaven.

They got there a good half hour ahead of everyone else. Johnny needed a word with Pennymaker about the business end of the ceremony, and when the hearse pulled in with the body in back he flagged it down.

"Stay there a minute, Daniel," he said. "I don't want the girls to be studying the box."

The two men went off by themselves a little ways. Three retired guys Pennymaker paid by the hour to shift the coffin and look grave—yes, a pun—stayed in the car and smoked.

The girls wandered among the headstones while they waited for Johnny. It might have been the first time either had ever been in a graveyard. Amy was going in beside Doc and Doc's sister Millicent. On Doc's stone there was a blank where Jeannine's name and birth date were already carved and under which she would be planted when it was her turn.

"Who was Millicent Weir?" Irene asked. Juny had a sense she wasn't supposed to talk about Millicent, though she wasn't sure why. That morning Juny had a feeling like she couldn't wake up.

"She was Doc's sister. She died when she was young."

"Was she married?"

"I'm not sure."

Irene looked at the dates on Millicent's stone: 1897-1928. She had been in the ground for longer than she'd been alive.

"I hope when people die," Irene said aloud, "they go to straight to heaven. I wouldn't want there to be something in between. That would be the only thing scary."

The earth where the mourners stood was muddy and mucked their shoes. They were there to put Amy's body in the ground and it was necessary that a little crowd be present when they did it. This time, unlike the last time they remembered Amy, this time there was hardly any of them there. Mrs. B came with Hodge, and Jeannine drove over alone. Roger Bottle took the morning off from his patients at the hospital.

Beside the hole in the ground there was a green tarpaulin covering the mound of earth the gravediggers had piled up. There was no service planned, not per se—what definition does the term "service" have without prayers and the rest of it? Probably some, but in any event Dr. Minor couldn't be there this time to preside. He was old and generally retired by then, and was spending more and more time at his sister's house down south in Savannah.

Abruptly Johnny observed that they were all looking to him, waiting for him to say something. He was suddenly shy. His mind drifted back to being called on in school.

"I don't pray," he said in a voice barely above a whisper, surprised that this was the first thing to come out of his mouth, "but I feel things I can't describe—things that aren't real but that make sense." He paused and tried to find a connector to the next thing. None came to mind.

"I guess there's a piece of mind for us in finally knowing, but it's sad all the same. I want to say that I miss Amy every moment of every day, and I always have. I feel the hole in the world that she left when she—when she left. But I would also like to say that I have felt Amy all around us from the day she went missing. She's never been far away. I think she sees us. I know how that sounds. There's nothing she can do, but I think she watches. I get feelings that she doesn't want us to be sad, that she wants us to think about our lives and living with one another. That from where she is she knows how hard it is for us just to live. That's the main reason I wanted to go through with all this today. Not to have grief for Amy but to remember her."

From the quiet of the others—who stared at the box with the body in it and stared at the hole in the earth—from their quiet Johnny thought he'd said something wrong or embarrassing. We don't always know what silence means.

Juny wasn't hearing anything anyhow. Today she doesn't remember what she was thinking; if it's possible to think about nothing she was thinking about nothing. To tell the truth she was pouting a little that morning. She had begged her father to see her mother's face in the box at the funeral parlor, and when Johnny told her no she cried. It was the only thing she cried about.

No one realized it for a moment but the extemporaneous ceremony ended when Johnny stopped speaking. The first of them to turn away was Jeannine. Then the others followed her out the cemetery gate to the shoulder of the road where their cars were parked. There was no reception for the mourners or anything like that. Not after what happened the last time.

Before driving off Jeannine turned and observed to Johnny, "I have an unhappy smell of drains at my house. Do you know what that might be?"

"Not without looking. I can come over tomorrow to see what the trouble is."

"That would be nice," Jeannine said. She looked some-how half surprised.

When he dropped around the next afternoon Johnny found his mother-in-law closed in thought. Peering in at the front window he saw Jeannine sitting in the dining room looking out on her backyard. In someone with a strong taste for privacy solitude can induce a type of trance. When Johnny rang the bell Jeannine put both hands on the arm of her chair and pushed herself up.

"You're as good as your word, John." He almost gagged when he came in. He knew the smell instantly.

"Good God, Jeannine, how can you stand that stink? Where's it coming from?"

"I think the kitchen. The past few days it got worse."

"That's at least one mouse." Johnny followed his nose to the back of the refrigerator and fished out the remains with a broom.

"I thought it was drains," Jeannine said as Johnny wheeled the thing away from him with disgust. Looking at that dead mouse on the end of the broomstraw made him ill.

"Give me room and I'll take this outside."

He flung the remains in the direction of the birdbath,

where sparrows splashed. A jay flew down from the trees to scare the sparrows and peck at the mouse; life goes on.

"I've been living with all the windows open." Jeannine was out the door behind him.

"You should have phoned me," Johnny said. Just to get the smell out of his nose he lit a cigarette. "Or even called Hodge. It was only a mouse, that thing."

"I didn't know that until just now." The subject had stopped being of interest to her. She lit her own cigarette.

Jeannine and Johnny never found conversation a pleasant thing if Juny wasn't around to buffer. For a full minute they stood awkwardly in the chilly shadow of the house with nothing to say.

"How have you been making out the past few days?" said Johnny, more to break the silence than for any other reason.

Jeannine shrugged. "About Amy? I find I'm not even sad. I'm not anything about it. More important is the question of Juny. How is she?"

"She doesn't say a lot. Unless I ask her straight out she hasn't told me anything."

"What have you asked her?"

"The things you'd expect, Jeannine. How does she feel? Was she scared? As far as I can tell she's OK. I don't trust it."

"Nor should you. Did you call the psychiatrist?"

"Not yet. I don't know what to say to him."

"Tell him your daughter came upon her mother's corpse and spent a sunny afternoon beside it. That should prick his interest."

After a long moment Johnny again asked Jeannine if she was bearing up.

"Peachy." She looked away from him, and then up at the empty sky. "It's hot."

"We'll sleep easier now."

Jeannine smiled at him.

"Do you feel better, John? Do you get anything from it?"

He knew the bitterness in her tone—it was familiar, just this side of a taunt—but he answered her anyway, almost in defiance.

"I do," he said. "All this time I had a clutched feeling in my chest—in my actual heart, I used to think. It hurt so much at times that I thought I should bring it up with Doc. Then this morning I was at a job and out of nowhere I noticed how I could take a full breath."

"You would have been smarter to ask Doc. Men are such mules when it comes to their health."

"I was hoping it would make you feel a little better, having Amy back."

"She's not back. She's dead." The undressed anger in Jeannine's voice was almost welcome for being direct. She flicked her cigarette toward the dead mouse and momentarily spooked the jay.

"Nothing is ever really a comfort," she said. "It's just that time goes by and things march along. I would like it to be finished now, is all."

Johnny gave her a sharp look and Jeannine laughed without smiling.

"Don't concern yourself, John. I'm not making plans to harm myself. To be honest it would make a nice change to feel a strong emotion like desperation."

Johnny looked over Jeannine's small face and searched

for physical resemblances to Amy. He wondered if after a few more years the detachment that teased him in Amy would have resolved itself into the family dismay, had she not died. Johnny would always be impressed by the Weir family's capacity for collapse.

"I'm glad having her body," he said.

Jeannine flinched at the word "body" and Johnny felt he had been rude. The only thing for it was to keep talking.

"It might be a bad thing to say, but mixed up in everything else after she disappeared was that my feelings were hurt. Stupid, I know, but the whole time I knew her I was never one-hundred percent sure that she was glad to be with me. That she meant it, if you know what I mean. Not that I thought she'd leave us, but there was a little part of me that did, like a little valve that turned off and on depending on which way I thought the wind was blowing for me. Stupid."

"People have such thoughts," said Jeannine. "Though I guess I should add that that's a fine thing to tell the mother."

It was summer essentially but things in that backyard were still covered with the leaves and twigs that came down during the previous winter. Jeannine hadn't yet taken a broom to the table and benches at the far end of her yard, which were covered in rusty pine straw. Her grass was unmowed; it must have been six inches high or more. Where they were standing in the shade of the house it was almost cold; Jeannine's bare arms prickled with gooseflesh. Just fifteen feet away there was sunshine, and yet the two of them stayed put. Johnny cleared his throat and was about to say good-bye when Jeannine spoke.

"What do you call a thought that won't leave your head?"

"I think that is what you call it."

"All I think about the last two days is Amy's body all rotten and falling apart. I have the most horrible images in my mind of worms and grinning teeth. I can't get the pictures out of my mind."

"She wasn't like that, Jeannine. She looked like herself."

"When I think about her in the grave I start imagining Doc down there with her too. All my loved ones rotting."

"What you liked about them isn't. And besides, not all of them are in the grave." Johnny was reaching for something kind to say, and he smiled.

"Thank you, John," said Jeannine, "but that gets the prize for emptiest comfort of all."

Consolation, of course, is not always a fraud. Still, what Jeannine said nagged at Johnny—not her meanness, to which he was accustomed, but her images of corruption. They crept into his own brain now and threatened to put down roots. It sent shivers through his frame when he thought of Juny being with the body in the riverside ooze. He shivered more when he asked if she stayed there with Amy all afternoon and Juny couldn't remember. "I think so," was all she told him. Her flatness scared him. He was only glad that Amy came to rest face down.

After visiting Jeannine that afternoon Johnny came back to the shop to telephone Dr. Stein and tell him the whole story.

"Happy."

"Happy?"

"That's the way I felt. I dug at the dirt with my stick for a while, but I was afraid to cut her so I told myself I'd better stop. I felt happy."

"Were you scared at all?"

"I wasn't. I wanted to make her turn over and look at me. I wasn't afraid of a monster face. I just wanted to see her." Juny had the feeling she was giving the wrong answers, the way she felt whenever a doctor asked her questions.

"It was like dreaming," she said. "I dream about mamma a lot, even before now. It always starts where I'm asleep."

"When you dream?"

"No, *in* the dreams. She gets me awake and we go out of the house."

"How do you know it's your mother in the dreams?"

"The way you know." This felt like a trick question. "I've seen pictures."

"What does she say?"

"She never says anything. I ask her and ask her. Sometimes in the dream I try to force my fingers in her mouth to stretch her teeth apart and make her talk. But she squeezes her lips together and won't say anything."

"Does that feel like she's being mean?" Juny shrugged. She didn't understand the question. No, of course it didn't.

"When you go out of the house in these dreams," Stein said, "where do you go?"

"Regular places."

"Tell me some. Because it's often the things we see out the corner of our eye during the day that make the biggest impression on our... On us. So when we sleep those things come out in dreams."

"We go all over. School. Down Bring Street. To the highway they're building. Up the Hill. It's like she's showing me around. Or sometimes it's like me showing her around. There's different moods."

"When you're with your mother in the dreams is it a happy feeling or what is it?"

"Not anything." Juny worried that the doctor was getting bored with her answers.

"Do your classmates ask you about your mother in school?"

"I think they talk about her, but I never do. I'm worried about my father."

"What's to be worried about with him?"

"Except for me he's lonely. And except for Office Meursault. She's the policewoman in Fortunes Neck. She's like his girlfriend, but really not. She comes around after they think I'm asleep and they make out on the porch. But they're not real lovey-dovey."

"Making out on the porch sounds like it's love-dovey."

"They're just helping each other."

"That's a funny way to put it."

"If you saw them you'd know."

"Does that bother you?"

"No."

"How about yourself—do you ever feel lonely?"

"I don't think so. Lots of times I wish I had my mother with us. I wish she was alive. That's not really lonely. It's more that I want to know about her—*real* things, not just how nice she was. I want to know what they all know."

"Who do you mean by 'they'?"

"My father and all of them."

In the outer office Mrs. Bliss was reading *Time* magazine. She was the one who drove Juny to Worchester at Dr. Stein's suggestion. Without the looming father figure, Stein explained to Johnny, the little girl might be less inclined to self-censor.

Later Stein mailed Johnny a bill for $35; we value what we pay money for. And he wrote this advice in a letter:

> *Dear Mr. Collins:*
>
> *What a pleasure it was meeting your daughter Juny the other morning in my office. She is a pleasing child, and I must say very concerned about you.*
>
> *This concern of hers should not worry you overmuch. Do not add it to your bag of apprehensions. It is common in children growing up in a worried household, and none could be more worried than a home from which the mother first disappears suddenly and now—under barely describable circumstances—is rediscovered by the very child who has longed for her return. It boggles an adult mind, and I can only guess at its effect on the thoughts of a little girl. And so I will guess.*
>
> *Your daughter, Mr. Collins, seems strong in a way that appears to be more than just toughness. Under normal circumstances (which these are certainly not) Juny would be at a difficult moment in her development. She is entering puberty, just to begin with. In addition to the initially dismaying physical changes this brings I would*

say she is beginning to lose what I think of as the double consciousness of childhood. You might define that as the willingness to accept the word of anyone taller than she is over the evidence of her own eyes. Now she is beginning to make her own estimations of events. But while yet without much experience in life she has only uncertain hunches about things. So do most adults, of course, but we are more used to it. Juny is acquiring a grown-up's awareness of reality's contradiction of her hopes. Unlike "successfully adjusted" grown-ups she has not yet learned to ignore the contradiction.

To my point about hunches, Mr. Collins, my assessment is that Juny is, in a deeply concentrated way, trying to make sense of a "complex" of disorganized impulses. She has never fully "displaced" her longing for her mother on to other adults—even on to you, I think. Try to imagine the tangle of her feelings—yearning for the mother, accepting the finality of the mother's extinguishment. Wanting to cry on your shoulder, afraid of doing anything that might add to your worries and further unsettle her home. What she needs is confidence that grief is not the end of happiness, confidence that she is part of a story with deep, constant roots and a long road still to go. She needs belief.

One practical suggestion I might offer is to spend time with Juny looking at your family photographs—especially those of her mother, of whom she is intensely (appropriately, in my judgment) curious. Tell her everything the pictures bring up in your mind; I suspect you will find this is of benefit in your own efforts to come to terms

*with this awful tale. Its benefit to your daughter may be
to illustrate the continuity of life even despite its broken
moments.*

*I know you have—and have had—a full load to carry
these past few years, Mr. Collins. But your daughter's
sense of security depends on believing that you have everything under control. Do so: Have everything under
control. Easier said than done, I realize.*

Yours sincerely,
Gerry Stein

A snapshot of Amy taken on the day she went missing
shows her in hot colors and carrying bolts of brilliant red
and yellow cloth across her arms—like she was carrying firewood, Johnny remembered thinking. That picture was the
first one he found. In their time together he and Amy always
meant to put their photographs in an album, but they never
did. Tomorrow never comes. After she disappeared Johnny
dumped all the photos in a shopping bag and after that forgot he owned a camera. Any pictures Juny has today of the
years after 1958 were all taken by someone else. All the snapshots from before that year were in the bag Johnny laid away
on the floor at the back of his bedroom closet. But on the
Sunday following Juny's visit to Dr. Stein her father dug the
photographs out and the two of them sat on the sunporch
looking through them and talking.

"In this one how old is she?" Juny asked that question
about half the time. She liked all the pictures of her parents
before there was her. She was uninterested in the monoto-
nous load of baby pictures showing her first in her father's

arms and then in her mother's.

"That's when she took the train to see me in Oklahoma—see the oil well in the back there? I posed her in front of that. She'd be about 19, I guess."

"She's looking away."

"She didn't feel well. I think she had the morning sickness that day. You can see from her stomach that it was about the time she was expecting you—see: she has a little belly. That's you in there."

They hauled the snaps out of the bag in handfuls and talked them over. Johnny was surprised by how much he'd forgotten.

"When was the first time you kissed her?"

"It's none of your business, little girl, but if I remember right it was walking home from a basketball game. I'm certain it was in the afternoon. The sun was out. Here's one we took the week we moved into the shop on Bring Street. Even then it needed paint—look."

"What did Mamma sound like?"

"She had a nice voice."

"What did it *sound* like?"

"Very pretty. Like the birds."

"Like Officer Meursault's?" This was an idea Juny had.

"No. Amy went up and down the scale when she talked. That's what I mean by like the birds. I wish I had a recording. There was something about her voice that sounded all the time like she was joking. It made me want to do anything I could think of to get her attention."

When Amy disappeared the first thing Johnny Collins told police in describing his wife was that she was smiling all the time. Johnny didn't say now, but he remembered how at some place in the inquiry into Amy's vanishing Johnny remarked to Ronald Meursault that Amy's way of smiling unsettled him. This aroused suspicions about him among the police, but it should not have. Amusement requires a remove from the thing that amuses, and Johnny was troubled by exactly that quality of detachment in Amy. He never understood what she found so funny. But the broad outline of our disposition is what people recall about us after we're gone.

"She was happy," he said, looking at the picture he held in his hand. "It's hard to explain. Once someone's gone the small things blow away from you. You don't ever think they will but they do." Juny did not believe him. She knew her father could play Amy's voice in his head whenever he felt like it.

"Here's one."

Amy by herself in the backyard of the house on Ploughman Road. The date stamp on the saw-tooth edge of the photograph is APRIL 1958. Even sitting in no-light at the bottom of the bedroom closet the color in the snapshot had nearly all blanched. In the shadow of the Weir's house Jeannine stands behind Amy, shielding her eyes against the sun like an Indian searching the horizon as she watches the picture taker. Her brother Hodge is also beside her, also squinting. The one side of Hodge's head is partly bald; only the week before he'd fallen asleep under a tanning lamp and nearly set fire to his hair. Amy stands in the foreground in petal-pushers and a sleeveless top. Around her throat is the red scarf she had just made for herself from leftover bits of rayon fabric, and her hair hangs straight down her back.

"I know this one," Johnny said. "We were over for Doc's

birthday so that would make it early spring. It was hot for that time of the year, but you can see there's no leaves on the trees yet. I remember this day. Everybody was in a fairly good mood for some reason. This would have been just before it happened."

"Why did you fall in love with her?"

"Well just look—you can see her how pretty she is." He handed the photograph to Juny and she looked. Even to a little girl Amy didn't look old enough to be a mother. The features of her face were still unfocused and her smile was cocky like a teenager's.

"At school she was in my class. I noticed her the whole way through, but in our last year I was pretty sure I'd be going in the army and I wasn't so dumb that I didn't expect some other guy would sweep her out from under me while I was away. That idea I didn't like at all. I remember one fella in particular named Chick that I was keeping my eye on. So I just made up my mind to get her as my girlfriend, and that I better move fast. That was the first time I ever worked it out that time goes by. It's funny how these ideas come to you."

That night, once Juny was in bed, Johnny sat with Lily out on the sunporch tossing through the bag of photographs. He had come across a shot of Ronald Meursault keeping order at the Memorial Day parade in 1955. He wanted Lily to have it. Remembering is contagious.

"I haven't told you," he said later on, "I haven't told you thank you for helping me when we found Amy. I wouldn't have wanted anyone else there but you."

"It was rough, the condition the body was in."

"That wasn't it so much. Not as much as it would have been if I knew ahead of time we were going to find her."

Lily nodded and shifted her weight against him. The night was so hung with humidity that the air felt oiled. They were naked and their flesh on flesh was rubbery, like wet baby-skin; without their feeling for each other the sensation would have been disagreeable.

"For you and me both I'm glad it wasn't horrible," Lily said.

"Jeannine told me last week that she can't stop thinking about the body. She said she was haunted by terrible pictures in her head of the way she looked. I tried to tell her it wasn't repulsive."

"People have those thoughts," said Lily, tucking her hip in closer to Johnny's. "It's very common," before adding, "Sad woman."

"Sad, yeah," Johnny said. "Talking to her brought back a thing I'd forgotten from then, that for months—and I mean for months, Lily—after Amy disappeared I was visited—you know, in my mind—by a picture I had of her in some awful place, some very small place. She was bloody all over, just red with it and in terrible pain, and nobody could hear her. It wasn't a nightmare. Middle of the day, walking down the street, it would come over me. If I didn't have Juny then to take me out of myself I don't know what would have happened."

"Maybe you knew something?"

Johnny considered the question.

"No," he said. "What could I have known?"

"Sometimes people know more than they think they do."

"No."

"Is that picture in your mind now? Right now?"

"Not unless I call it back."

"Well, there you go. Don't call it back."

They were quiet. The wheedle of crickets surrounded them. They were in the deep summer night.

"The moment she hit her head Amy was gone from the earth," he said. "Once I could finally take that in then afterward—being dead—the rest of it was nothing to me. Still, Lily, I appreciated that you were gentle with her. That's all I'm saying."

"It was only respectful."

"You were good at your job."

"Thank you. I was never in quite that position before. I've handled the dead but nothing like that. If I didn't take it easy I didn't know what would have happened. And it was your wife. It was hard not to have feelings about it."

"I appreciate that."

"That night after I got home," she told him, "when I washed my hands that night the funniest feeling came over me that we had done something wrong." Lily's warm breath was pleasant across the skin of Johnny's shoulder when she spoke. "It was as if we had disturbed a grave, if you follow that. I was glad it was you holding the light for me and not some County guy. They can be kind of coarse."

"I hope you don't still have that feeling now."

"Of disturbing her?" she said. "No. That stopped."

Johnny stretched for his cigarettes and was careful not

to make Lily shift again; affection shows itself in these tiny ways. He struck a match, and down the dark hallway in the kitchen Juny loved the look of her father's face in the little firelight.

"Amy wanted us to bring her out," he said. "If I have any feelings about it at all it's how lonely she must have been. Seven years there underwater. That bothered me, I'll admit."

"You're better now?"

"My foot's asleep." He swung his legs over and sat up straight without letting go of Lily. She pulled herself up higher on his shoulder and hung on.

"Amy would have liked you," Johnny said.

"Keep dreaming. I'm sure she would not have liked me canoodling with you out on her sunporch."

"Maybe, maybe not. I never knew about anything for sure with Amy."

"It was the father put her off of me."

"I won't argue."

"What was eating at him? He was always being so churly."

"Doc? I could no more tell you why than tell you the name of the man in the moon. When it's my turn to die that's on my list of things I want to ask about if I get to the other side. That's how I picture it, people talking over what they didn't understand here on earth."

"And having a laugh."

"Why do you think it'll be laughs?"

"Because they'll be all stored up."

Lily rolled out from under his arm and pinned him to the couch.

"Lie still," she said. "My appetite is wet."

Whatever it is they do in heaven Johnny found out three years later, in 1968.

It was November again and he was driving home from an emergency job at a restaurant in Lordshaven. Riding down the hill to the Bring Street Bridge his wheels skidded on a thatch of wet leaves. He hit the brakes and the car slid into the retaining wall of the old bridge. It wasn't much of a crash but it propelled him into the windshield and cracked his head.

Just from the sound of it a woman one street over knew someone had wrecked. She telephoned the Meursaults and Lily picked up. It happened that she had been about to drive over to Cottage Row.

Once she got to the bridge Lily radioed for an ambulance. Ignoring the dozen or so watchers who'd appeared from nowhere to come and see the accident she climbed into Johnny's car, on the passenger side, and waited there.

It turns out that in every moment we inhabit several places at once.

"If you think about it," Johnny Collins used to say, "behind everything there's a system." But his dying argued the other way. Nothing foreshadowed his death. It was out of the blue and it led nowhere but the cemetery. Juny never changed her idea about that. Johnny left behind only his absence, and that for eternity. Eternity has no system.

Like everyone else on Earth Juny tried to read the events in life as a long story, in which one thing led to another; fat chance of that ever happening. When her mother disappeared all the adults had conspired to help her believe that the world had a logic, that events weren't just events but consequences. But when her father died they were all too tired to argue about it anymore.

Two days later Johnny was buried. For the burial they were all there but for Lily Meursault, who declined to come. Her mother phoned up Mrs. Bliss to explain.

"My daughter feels this will be one of those things better left to family," Mrs. Meursault said.

"I had an idea Mr. Collins felt about Office Meursault as if she was family."

"It isn't me you need to convince about that, dear, if you know what I mean."

"I do," said Mrs. B.

Johnny's body was in a plain walnut casket just like the one Daniel Pennymaker sold him for Amy. Pennymaker's showroom was full of that model. Jeannine Weir's brother Laurence came down from Vermont with his wife to attend the burial. They stood with Amy's headstone at their feet. Standing on the opposite side of the hole in the ground where Johnny was going to be buried were Hodge and Mrs. Bliss. Juny stood with them. That morning she wore a short black skirt; it was chilly and her knees were red. Juny was shaky inside. So many eyes on her made her feel like she might jump. She pictured herself levitating, lifting off, going away over the hills, just to please be left alone.

The morning was cold and clear. One could see for miles, maybe as far as Agawam. The trees were mostly bare by then, moulding. The bark on the trees was black with wet. Their red and orange leaves were turning brown on the ground. The leaves blew into the hole dug by Pennymaker's men.

"Hodge," said Mrs. B. "Would you like to say something?"

Hodge smiled the way he would at a customer expressing an interest in Bermuda.

"Well," he said. "I wish Johnny was here to speak for himself, but it looks like we're on our own. I knew I'd be asked to make remarks this morning—it isn't that I'm unprepared—but I've not come up with anything to sum it up. Johnny's life, I'm saying. So I'll relate a story that Amy once told me. When they were in high school one time Johnny comes by the house to pick Amy up for a date. Typical of him he arrives early. He's just lifting his fist to knock on our screen door when he hears my father saying inside the house 'John is all right as far as he goes, but where will he ever take you?'" Hodge lowered his voice to a baritone when he impersonated his father, although in life Doc had a tenor voice that might have been called fluty. "Do you remember that one, mother?"

"No," said Jeannine. You never knew what Jeannine was thinking.

In fact, Hodge remembered that it was his mother who'd made that remark about Johnny, but he'd change the attribution to avoid putting her on the spot. "I guess we'll all remember different things about those days in our own ways," he told them. "My point is anybody else would have had their feelings hurt to hear themselves talked about that way, or been embarrassed by it. Amy said Johnny *was* a little bit, but really he didn't care. He was going to get my sister and my father could just go to hell about it. I think he was smart."

Hodge could not have been more pleasant. He looked like a hunted man.

"The main things is I don't know why this has happened. Johnny certainly didn't have this coming. But I know for a fact if he were here he'd have something to say about it. He liked living, in spite of everything."

"Amen," said Jeannine, whether in agreement or to head Hodge off from saying anymore. Then the rest of them said amen's. It felt like the appropriate thing to do.

Juny didn't hear any of what her uncle was saying. For two days she'd been absorbed in a memory that repeated in her head the way a melody sometimes will. It must have been from the months after her mother disappeared. Whenever it was, she and her father were alone in the house. She was very small and her father seemed very big. For some reason he lifted her on to the toecaps of his big black shoes and began waltzing her around their kitchen. His eyes were all on her.

The way she remembered it his face was shining. Bending from the waist his breath probably smelled of coffee. They tango'd and they waltzed. Johnny was singing to her.

And he walks with me
And he talks with me
And tells me
I am his own.

Twenty years later Juny was at a Congregationalist funeral and they sang that one. It was no love song but a holy hymn. But where would her father have learned a hymn? Not in church, where he seldom had a reason for going. And not from his Aunt Margaret. She was an acrimonious atheist. But the day they buried him Juny stood in front of the box that had her father lying in it and heard his voice singing in her head.

Even then—13 years old, black skirt—she understood that this was less a memory of her father than of herself. From now on everyone would care for her, but what she wanted was the expression on her father's face when he looked her way. To whom was the fact of her just a pleasure anymore? Now she would be one care among many. Juny was frightened to watch her idea of herself flicker.

This was all in the week of November when winter arrives. It was cold that night of the funeral, and the next morning they woke up to rain. Juny was made to go school; they'd consulted Dr. Stein and he thought the immediate reestablishment of routine would be for the best. Juny didn't care what she did.

It was clear already that she was going to be living with

her Uncle Hodge and Mrs. Bliss in the house next door to her old home. Juny lived there with them three years. It was a surprise to Hodge and Mrs. B, finding themselves in that role. For Juny they bought clothes, got her up for school, watched over her, gave her pocket money, played the part of parents. They had no gift for it but they did all the right things.

It would not be until she left Fortunes Neck and all its associations that Juny stopped feeling not orphaned but fatherless. There was not a morning in her high-school time when she didn't wake up thinking about her father. As a grown woman she still dreams of her mother from time to time. But her father is always in the frame, waving from the afterlife.

In American movies the best part is always the moment just few minutes from the end, the moment when everyone hugs and the whole thing is made clear at last. But in Juny's life there always seemed to be one thing more she was supposed to hear about.

That first year after her father died was a year of real-estate. Bob Trammel was hired to manage the sale of both Collins P&H and the house on Cottage Row—the house where Johnny had been raised by his Aunt Margaret and where years later he raised Juny. The money from those sales—$53,000—waited for Juny in a savings account until she grew up. Her old house was bought by a newlywed couple named Case.

Juny wanted little out of the house when they sold it for her. Her things—clothes and so forth, the bag of snapshots kept in the hall closet (which she'd only ever once sorted through). The nostalgia reflex is primitive in a 13 year-old. And the Cases were newly wed, needing everything—they bought the furniture, the kitchen things and so on, even her father's tools. Today all Juny regrets are the tools.

"They've taken a shine to you," Mrs. Bliss told Juny on the same day Mr. and Mrs. Case moved in. You wouldn't know that from Mr. Case, who was not unfriendly but spoke to people even less than Uncle Hodge. Mr. Case was a fanatic gardener, hacking and digging in the ground every spare moment. His wife, on the other hand, Mrs. Case, didn't have a job and was around the house all day. Mrs. Case was about 30 or maybe a bit older, and she seemed to know all about Juny's story. Trammel probably mentioned it as a strategy for getting Mr. and Mrs. Case to sweeten their offer on the house. He was merciless that way.

"I want you to always feel welcome in your former home, Juny," Mrs. Case said. "Come by anytime you want to talk about things. We can be like sisters."

Juny had no wish for a sister. But some people are born with more affection in them than the world wants. That was Mrs. Case. When Juny walked down the street she never knew if Mrs. Case would pop from behind a parked car or out from under the tulip tree on the front lawn, where the all-night birds still went on nattering, indifferent to who was living in Juny's old house. Sometimes Mrs. Case called to her across the yards. She would stand hidden in the shadows of the sunporch, where Johnny used to be in the evenings with

Lily Meursault. Mrs. Case made a point of speaking to Juny like an adult, which is tedious for an adolescent. Mrs. Case was aching to be pregnant and gave Juny all the details.

Then in the spring Gramma Jeannine sold her house on Ploughman Road and moved back Vermont. "I'm completing a circle," she told Roger Bottle. Jeannine took a house near her brother Laurence and his wife, and before long she started going with Laurence to an older-people's Bible class called "Homework for Immortality." Juny never heard a word from her except for phone calls on her birthdays and for Christmas.

Hodge Weir had fallen all out of touch with his mother even before she moved away. In the old days when Johnny was alive Jeannine sometimes visited on Cottage Row, but she never once went next door to see her son when he was living with Mrs. B—not a single time that Juny remembers; it's amazing the things people will do to each other and expect there to be no consequences. After Juny went to live next door she saw how awkward it was for Uncle Hodge those rare times that her grandmother phoned to wish her happy birthday or something like that and Hodge had the bad luck to pick up the telephone. His end of these exchanges was painful to watch. He spoke in a voice that sounded like he owed money to the person on the other end of the line.

One time Juny asked Mrs. Bliss if she thought Jeannine was angry at Hodge.

"Not at Hodge," Mrs. Bliss answered. "Not per se. At something, though, and Hodge is the magnet for it."

"Why?"

"I couldn't tell you, pet. Maybe nothing and I'm wrong.

But if you're asking, living alone the last few years has made Jeannine funny. She was a bit that way before, of course, but when Doc died he left her friendless. Take my word for it, so much solitude makes an odd duck out of you. It puts your attention on all the wrong places. No wonder Jeannine's gotten to be like a dog that doesn't know it's own pup."

Hodge and Mrs. Weir had lost their points of connection, if they ever had them. The thought brightened in Juny that Gramma Jeannine was like Uncle Hodge and he like her; it was his inheritance from her. Both of them were like people walking with their heads down. By such flashes of illumination we feel our way forward.

Ａll her life Juny Collins has kept her eyes open for correlations, for connections in the evidence. From an early age her impulse was to assemble a narrative from data; she has never completely abandoned that project. Her first job out of college would be as an actuary for a Boston insurance firm. Her specialty was the assessment of non-traditional risk; there is no end of ways to spend one's time.

As an actuary Juny liked how the story that numbers told was both real and at the same time the arrangement she made of them. Working out whether it was one or the other used to absorb her mind all day long. Friends would ask her to use actuarial tables to predict things—the likelihood of an early death for someone they despised, say, or chances of that person's dismemberment. Juny reminded them that she could not forecast outcomes for any individual, only for categories of individual. That didn't stop people from asking. Everyone wants to know the future. It's the same all over.

Who knows how but by the time she was in high school it was apparent that Juny had this feel for numbers. In class her mind wandered over equations chalked by the teacher on the blackboard—not just the solution but within and among the numbers. It was like daydreaming for her. Each numeral appeared to tell its personality, or the quality instinct to it. Juny had one theory that prime numbers were regal; they were so self-sufficient. A good example was 3. And yet 5 was gentle and democratic, even mystic, and 7 was a straight arrow, a prince if you know him and really the least square. None of it was just one thing, unmixed—*although* 8 was smug because she was so tight with 9, the sedulous sister. 10 Juny just felt sorry for. 10 was an old woman with too much to do, carrying the world on her back like that tortoise in mythology, uncomplaining.

In sophomore year Juny learned how to do graphs. That tipped her perspective permanently. Anything through time, it turned out, could be plotted on x and seen in its relation to y. The long reach of history could show its motif.

Once Juny was in the public library and found a stack of booklets from the National Weather Service reprinting tables of climate data for Massachusetts starting in 1917. She had the bright idea of finding the total precipitation in the months when her parents and Doc died; she remembered rain in April, 1958, and November, 1968, and snow for January, 1961. She plotted them against the normals, a word she never encountered before that day; she liked saying it. The trend lines were almost identical. They demonstrated nothing. Same thing with mean temperatures.

Juny mentioned her findings—or rather the lack of any—to Irene, who had her own taste for data.

"What all those things have in common," Irene replied instantly, "is that in each of those years a musical won the Academy Award for best picture."

"What does that prove? Musicals must have got Oscars in other years but nobody I know personally died then." Juny found Irene's suggestion banal, a word she had just discovered and liked for the way it sounded sophisticated and put things at a distance—a perfect word for adolescence.

"And those would be the outliers," Irene replied. But Juny knew events cause facts and not the other way around. Correlations are not evidence. Not all patterns can be summed.

Junior year she was assigned a project on local history. She decided to write something about local population trends. She mailed a letter to Dr. Bottle, grandpa Doc's old partner at Peconic Hospital, asking to study the birth and death records for the 50 years between 1920 and 1970. She would like to see what they revealed.

"You're not preparing a malpractice suit, are you, Juny?" Bottle asked her when he returned her call a few days later. He was joking.

"I'd like to find if there are patterns over time," Juny replied, and then surprised herself by adding, "if I could see whether the years my parents and Doc died were departures from the normals."

"I can fix it for you to get a look at the raw numbers," Bottle said, "though I'm not aware that we add 'em up at the end of every year. I can find out. I would challenge your methodology, though. A lot of people have moved to this area in the last 30 years, and people are mainly on the young side when they move house so a lot of babies will get born subsequently. The population averages younger, so the death rate goes down, more or less. Even though the numbers of deaths might stay relatively constant on average. That would be true even if people live longer. But eventually they've all gotta go."

"What does that prove?" Juny asked. She was taking

notes for her school project now.

"It doesn't prove anything," Bottle told her. "Except people die no matter what year it happens to be. For everybody involved it's a very big thing when it happens to them personally. But that's not science," he said, joking again, "that's psychology. Or say it another way, that's subjectivity."

"Our assignment is describe something and leave the subjectivity out."

"Gosh. High school is a lot harder than it used to be. I guess the problem with data like what you're after, not that I've thought much about it, is that it's *just* numbers, if you see what I mean. In the aggregate they something, yes they do. But they tell nothing much about the choices people make that *determined* their morbidity and mortality. If you could collect that information you'd have a prize-winning term paper."

"Our assignment is unearth patterns."

"Very logical. I'd also find a way to write a little about accident, events that don't fit a pattern. All of this is kept by the County. If you come up empty let me know. The legal category is probably 'death by misadventure'. There's probably no 'birth by misadventure', though that's a ripe idea."

"Like my mother."

"Like your mother, um hmm. Actually, another interesting topic for you would be to ask why they change the way they define their terms every few years. You'd think that much would be settled anyhow."

"Do you think my mother died by accident?"

Dr. Bottle paused, and when he spoke again Juny noticed a more level tone in his voice, as if he wanted to be very sure she had no doubt that her mother died by accident.

"From all I read and heard and was told, Juny, there was no doubt about it. If you can understand me, dear, don't afflict yourself with doubt."

"There are just things I want to know."

"I understand."

"Dr. Bottle, did you deliver me when I was born?"

"I did."

"Do you remember my mother?"

"I'd like to say I do, Juny, but it was more than 15 years ago. A lot of what I might tell you I probably only think I remember. There's that subjectivity again."

"Can you try?"

"There isn't much. She had a small fame but she was strong, physically. She was very close to your father, and I'm not making that up to please you. He came along to her office visits, and I remember that because most men don't see the need. And I recall clearly, because I was asked about it at the time, how she seemed to me when I examined her the morning the day she went missing."

Juny felt her insides fall.

"You saw her that day?"

"Yes."

"Why?" And again she heard Dr. Bottle pause.

"She was expecting the baby. Don't let this upset you, Juny. Maybe I shouldn't be revisiting this with you."

"I'm not upset, sir."

"Your mother was full of life that day. Literally, she was full of life."

"Did my father come with her that time to your office?"

"No. That was the day she found out for sure. She hadn't told him yet. Juny?"

"Yes."

"I assumed your family knew. Your grandfather knew. He must have told your father."

"Daddy didn't know. He would have said something to me."

"He must have."

"He didn't."

"Well, if so maybe he was trying to protect you."

"From what?"

"From knowing?"

"Was my mother happy about it?"

"Of course. Women are always happy about it when they're going to be mothers. Actually that isn't true. Your mother was anxious about some things, but women get anxious."

"Can you tell me what she was anxious about, please?"

"Normal things. Physical worries she had. Some concern about the extra expense of a new baby. It's sort of private, Juny, even at this late date. In a way Amy is still my patient."

"But she felt better after she left you?"

"Left my office? Sure. I'm a good doctor."

"Thank you, Doctor. Goodbye for now."

Hanging up the telephone Juny was conscious of a pins-and-needles sensation in the world. This is a skull's response to the penetration of a large new thing: a brother. a sister. Certainly Juny didn't want a new sister. In that role she could not help casting Irene Horn, so no thank you. Picturing a brother was the same as imagining cities on other planets, imagining other planets at all. After a while the mind just stops.

Of greater wonder to Juny was whether her father knew what the others knew—Dr. Bottle, Grandpa Doc, Officer Meursault, her mother. Her father. Would her father have been glad, stupid from glee like a father on television? And where would that leave her? Jealousy was not familiar to Juny. Her father always gave Juny protection from that. She was never jealous of Lily, nor of her mother (thinking of this now for the first time, and feeling the ground move a little on that one—what if her mother had been like Mrs. Horn, banal? Juny knew the world she knew. That it could have been otherwise felt the same as imagining a lover with anyone besides ourselves. We would ask, How is such a thing even desirable?)

In Juny's last year of high school Uncle Hodge brought her to the Father/Daughter Ball. That night there was a band playing rock-and-roll and swing music both; it was an evening of truce between the fathers and daughters. Around her head that night of the ball Juny tied a scarf with a paisley pattern. She looked like a small-town Apache. She wore a short suede skirt that she knew made her uncle uneasy. Uncle Hodge never knew what the limits of his authority were with her, and she was not above exploiting his uncertainty. Rulings on skirt lengths were a good example.

The other girls' fathers, men with pink scraped cheeks, noticed Juny standing apart with her uncle, not dancing.

With the formality of men uneasy in their good clothes they asked Hodge for permission to box-step his niece around the floor; such small kindness is everywhere. Juny in their arms they danced, joshing with her more than they would had they met her on the street. It was because they were embarrassed by her growing up. Through the back of her blouse her heat glowed, heat they didn't notice when they danced their own daughters.

When they returned Juny to her uncle the men stopped a moment to chat. Under their affability was the interest Hodge Weir forever attracted almost without moving. Hodge with all his reputations: killer, business-owner, Doc's son, free-lover. Hodge was the travel agent for most of these people and he made himself congenial. But he would not take a turn on the dance floor.

"Forbidden," he joked when they goaded him. "Order of the fire marshal."

"Get on out and waltz with your niece," one man teased him when toward the end of the evening the band played "Snowfall".

"All right," Hodge said at last, throwing up his hands in mock resignation, "all right, but later you'll be sorry."

This was the same gymnasium where Hodge used to dance with Mrs. Bliss 25 years before, which in the span of things is not long. Hodge's feet remembered the dance steps. But Juny felt his resistance to the three-four waltz-beat in the stickman's way he held her. Uncle Hodge was no use to her at all in imagining what it would be like to be held by a grown man. She had only a little idea of what it was like to be held by any kind of man at all; her short record of high-school romance could not even be called mixed. The boys she'd had dates with were all over-curious about her knotted story, and it closed her up. Juny was 17 years old and already the weeds of her history were annoyingly high.

"I don't want to talk about it," she would tell the boys if they asked questions. "It's boring," she'd say. Of course to outsiders it was anything but. It was almost more intriguing to the boys than getting Juny to walk with them down the Watermeadow. If she said she wouldn't go with them they'd ask her, "Is it… because of what happened?"

Like anyone her age Juny half wished to be invisible. In Fortunes Neck that would be impossible, the same as it used to be for the rest of them back when everyone was alive. Among other things Juny's guardian killed a woman once. No one ever forgets a story like that, never fully.

In senior year Irene Horn found a boyfriend, Tim House. Putting Tim in the picture opened a distance between Juny and Irene, whose daydreams now and monologues were mainly on the theme of love's transports. Tim used to be one of the boys stalking girls down along the river back in eighth grade. "That was a long time ago," Irene argued when Juny brought this up. About the time the Father/Daughter ball was ending Irene was sneaking out of the house to meet Tim down at the Bring Street Bridge. Juny thought of them as she collected her coat, though not with envy. Mystification was closer to it. Tim was a starting guard on the football team, big but to Juny's eye not even handsome.

Romance was in season that spring not only for Irene but for her mother too. Mrs. Horn had fallen for Jack Parsons. Or rather *he* had fallen for *her*. One afternoon Parsons was coming down Bring Street from his insurance office when for no reason he folded up and fell down. He was unconscious a moment, and when he looked up he was staring into the face of Irene's mother. Sunshine in the blue sky that day created the effect of a halo around Mrs. Horn's head. Parsons would forever be sentimental about that. He was always a great one for signs.

"What happened to *you*?" said Mrs. Horn. She folded her sweater and tucked it under his head as he lay on the sidewalk.

"I'm not sure what happened," Parsons told her. "But there's the funniest feeling in my chest, like a bird is fluttering under my ribs."

Parsons hadn't spoken to Mrs. Horn for eight years, not since he renovated the kitchen of her house on Cottage Row in 1964. But he'd seen her around. He remembered with tenderness how they used to talk in the afternoons when she came in from work and he'd be tidying up. Completely unknown to Mrs. Horn, Parsons had been carrying a small torch for her ever since. He had kept her in his heart and now they were reunited. It was like the movies.

The following Sunday was Easter. Parsons phoned Mrs. Horn and asked if he might take her to breakfast to say thank-you for helping him that day when he collapsed.

"All I did was roll your eyes back," she told him. It was a nurse's sort of joke.

"But it meant a lot to me," he said.

Easter morning Parsons came by to take the ladies to church. After that they were going for breakfast at the Bring Street Café.

"I don't know why we have to go to church," Irene told Juny. "It's not like we do it all the time."

That morning Hodge Weir came out of his house at the same time Parsons appeared with Irene and her mother, all of them dressed in their Easter clothes. Hodge was in slacks and a sweater vest. He was on his way over to Bring Street Grocery to buy milk and eggs for Sunday breakfast. Automatically he called out "Good morning!" to the neighbors when he saw them. Irene and her mother returned Hodge's greeting. But Jack Parsons glowered; all his hope of Easter renewal was gone. As for Hodge, he walked almost all the way to the grocery before realizing who the other man was.

Mr. Parsons and Mrs. Horn went together nearly a year. It was a low-profile romance. Low profile not really because Mr. Parsons was a suspect character but because of Mrs. Horn. She was always conscious of being a divorcée and was afraid of what people would whisper if they saw her out publicly with a man—any man, not just Parsons.

"When you've had a broken marriage," she told Mrs. Bliss, "people will always look at you like you were the bootlegger's daughter."

There's an assumption everyone shares that ardor should be respected, as if it were a noble character trait. This doesn't make any sense and we all know it. Mr. Parsons was instantly ardent with Mrs. Horn. It started with the roses he sent her after taking the ladies to breakfast on Easter morning. Then he got Mrs. Horn to agree to dinner—just them—during which he mentioned that a friend had given him three spare tickets to a baseball game down in New Britain; that was an odd number of tickets to fall into someone's lap. Anyway, Parsons persuaded Mrs. Horn that she and Irene would enjoy themselves. In fact, they did, especially Mrs. Horn, who liked baseball and loved being outdoors at the ballpark. It was fun for her, doing things with Parsons. For almost 12 years she'd had no man to accompany her, and just about this time she saw herself succumbing to drudgery, to some lifelong slump. She feared what it would be like for her once Irene left the nest, and the time was coming soon.

One evening that summer, when Irene and Juny were at the movies, Mrs. Horn noticed Mrs. Bliss sitting out on her front steps having a smoke. Hodge had gone to bed. Mrs. Bliss came across the street to say good evening.

"How are you tonight?" Mrs. Horn said politely.

"Tonight I miss Casey," Mrs. Bliss replied. But Mrs. Horn—who shared her daughter's indifference to dogs—had come to talk about Jack Parsons and she got down to it as soon as she'd borrowed a cigarette.

"He means to be awfully sweet," she said, "I realize he does, and God knows he's been through enough to turn anyone sour. I've heard all about it, believe me, from Jack himself and what he doesn't tell me people at the hospital are delighted to fill in the details. My goodness, we live in a fishbowl, no matter how hard we try living on the q-t. I feel sorry for Jack because I understand that. I know what it's like to want to believe in the hearts and flowers. But he overdoes it. I don't even like chocolate. I'm sorry if I sound mean—not mean, I'm not saying that. Really he's not at all scary in the way I'm saying, even Irene is warming up to him, I think. But he can be so awful quiet, the way men are, until he gets going. Things haunt him, you know? Although most of the time he does live in the present. But he remembers that big fire all right. Poor guy, it was the biggest thing that ever happened to him and it was over 20 years ago. He's been carrying his mixed-up ideas about Hodge's family for so long that I think he doesn't remember what for. He took me out to the drive-in a week ago and on the way home he goes by Eden Hills so he could show me where his place used to be. It's people's homes now, I told him, they'll get the County cops on us if we go prowling around. But he had to have a look and tell me where his barn used to be, what he used to plant over there, how his little girl used to play in the kitchen garden. It was poignant, I guess. But why go back? For me he's full of sweet-nothings. I know it's all about the wife even more than it is about the daughter, if you're asking me, and who he's never allowed to see. It's the trouble he has living with his memory. Being off to himself has turned his thoughts all around, and darkened them. That's what this is all about, what he says he feels for me. That's what it's always about whenever you hear people saying they fell in love, really. He was just waiting for something in high heels to come along. We love what we want someone else to be for us. Jack wants me to be his recompense to the past, but it can't be done. I'm 42, for Pete's sake."

Juny seldom saw Mr. Parsons come by the house to pick up Mrs. Horn, but once in a while he materialized out of the Horns' front door on a Sunday morning.

"He snores," Irene confided to Juny. It was hard to tell if Irene liked or disliked Mr. Parsons, but she was definitely dismayed by his lack of panache. She was expecting more.

Then in September Parsons turned to Mrs. Horn one night and said, "I'd like to be a father to Irene." The Horns had a sunporch too.

Afterward Mrs. Horn would always be nagged—but only a little—by the idea that her alarm at the idea of marriage to Parsons had shown too obviously in her face. She had no wish to cause Parsons more pain, but no, she said, no, she could not. Marriage had burned her.

At eleven o'clock the dance ended and Mrs. Bliss came to collect Hodge and Juny. On the drive home the three of them said hardly a word. The ball was over, it was fun—what else was there to say about it?

Juny sat alone in the back seat. It was a short ride home from school across the Bring Street bridge to Cottage Row. The moon was full that night and lit the bare trees in silhouette; lots of them had broken limbs from storms the previous winter. Juny rolled down the car window to let in the moist spring air. The night was more than chilly, it was cold. Most of us have nose enough to sniff hope in the month of April. It's in that faint scent of bread dough that comes up out of the earth, that discernable thing.

Mrs. Bliss had her hair in a perm that spring. It gave her skull a sprung silhouette as she sat behind the wheel of the car as she drove them home. That hairdo made Mrs. B look

15 years older than she was, which was 49. She and Uncle
Hodge talked about interesting things less than they used to,
though Mrs. B did not seem unhappy. Happy/not-happy appeared to have nothing to do with it. She lived with Hodge
in what Juny imagined as a perfect sphere of connection.

Back in history, Juny knew, Gramma Jeannine had discouraged romance between Mrs. Bliss and Uncle Hodge.
That story wasn't hard to piece together; Mrs. B was always
dropping clues about it for as long as Juny could remember. Mrs. Bliss waited a long time for her victory over Mrs.
Weir. It seemed almost that she cared more about making
that point than she did about wanting Uncle Hodge himself;
people do such things and do them all the time. Mrs. Bliss
treated Hodge kindly, but she had treated her dog Casey
kindly too. Juny had no idea what they had between them, or
what they talked about that was private between adults. She
had an image of them as two hands with threaded fingers, all
locked in. To Irene she referred to them as "the lovebirds",
when she referred to them; now and then she liked to give
Irene something to work with. In a certain light their arrangement could look like the ideal of romance, Hodge coming home every night to the bunker of their history; imagine
that phrase in a love-song.

> *I live for the solace*
> *Of her kiss for me*
> *I shelter in the bunker*
> *Of our history.*

Perhaps not. But after Casey died Mrs. B adopted an
unchristened cat, and like that cat Uncle Hodge appeared

to know things without understanding them. The sensations piled up.

When Jeannine Weir died they brought her body back from Vermont to be buried with Doc in Mount Hope Cemetery. As his mother's will required, Hodge carved his mother's lament for Amy on the headstone:

...the dead tree gives no shelter, the cricket no
relief,
And the dry stone no sound of water.

Mrs. Bliss outlived Jeannine Weir by barely eight months. She was young when she died—just 54, of chondrosarcoma that began in her arms. But Mrs. B stuck around long enough to win her argument. There was probably no meaning in it when after she died Hodge put her in the ground between Jeannine and where he would be planted when his own turn came; Hodge was never known to be vindictive.

When Hodge took his turn in 1987—the last of them to die unless you want to count Lily Meursault—he was snuggled in to the Weir family plot close to his sister Amy and to Johnny. Once Hodge joined them it was crowded underground. Johnny Collins had the outside position, though a lot he probably cared about that since he got to lie beside Amy. Doc's sister Millicent would always have the best spot, nearest the graveyard fence, under a tree, because she went in first.

In September Juny was starting at the University of Massachusetts in Boston. That was as far away from Fortunes

Neck as she could get and still qualify for in-state tuition. She nursed a private idea of what the city would become for her. Her aim was that she would turn seriously pretty. And taller. Juny was as good in biology as she was in math, and she had learned enough about inheritance to hope there might be a mislaid gene for tallness on her father's side. Her father had not been particularly tall, but the few photographs she'd seen of her great Aunt Margaret suggested possible ambitions for height. On her mother's side the Weirs were people of only average size; Juny found no encouragement there. All the Weirs seemed to pass down was a talent for regret, a trait. Juny worried that it might even be ticking away in her.

Sometimes she used to wonder if it might be better for the world if she never had children. Except that every woman she'd ever met was a mother. But for Mrs. Bliss and Officer Meursault; and they didn't seem too bad off about it. Though they were oddball in certain ways. Lily Meursault Juny only saw by chance now, if she bumped into her on the sidewalk or the time when Lily gave the lecture on traffic safety to the driver's education class. Juny exchanged hellos if ever they met, although she was never convinced that Lily remembered who she was. Juny was a young woman now, and wore glasses.

That night of the dance was when Juny first imagined that she need not be the product of her genes or of her history, that she could be the thing that happened. That was how she put to herself: "the thing that happened". Juny believed she could change tendencies. There was no evidence to support this idea but visions come to us because we call them. Juny's vision was of giving everyone the slip. That night of the ball she saw how when summer ended she would never live in Fortunes Neck again, and so escape her fate. She never would, and she did.

"Don't look down," she told herself as this idea gained on her, "don't look down or your nerve will go." It was an act of faith she was making, the closest thing to a conversion experience she ever knew.

Back when everybody was alive Juny always wondered at how a few of them—Mrs. Bliss, say, or her father—seemed to find something of interest wherever they looked and the rest of them—which meant the Weirs, essentially—did not. Juny never decided if it was a difference in point of view or something physical in the brain. But there must to be something willed about joylessness because the opposite seems so ready to break out in people all the time.

Juny's first few years in Boston after college were awkward and sometimes forlorn. She had no talent for the social wheel. Even before she left Fortunes Neck she was beginning to feel hobbled by her clumsiness at small talk. Juny liked to think of herself as direct and the majority of us know that most conversation is idle.

In those first years in Boston there wasn't much that took Juny's interest except for being an actuary and of course the story of her mother and her father and the Weirs and Irene and Lily Meursault. Most of the time that was a story she was shy about telling. A storyteller needs a trustworthy listener, and Juny has found so few of them. Sometimes people responded with curiosity, and then they always asked too many questions. Other times they treated Juny's history as something merely personal. Whichever it was made her irritable, and so easily that for a long time Juny suspected she might be tough to get along with.

After college she moved to an apartment house in the Back Bay. It was a dark five-floor walk-up that roasted the tenants in summer and smelled of insecticide all year long. The day she moved in she was carrying an armload of boxes and a man living there named Marshall House held the front door open for her. Marshall lived on the floor below Juny's. He was an easy man, untroubled, a salesman for Southern New England Telephone. And he was instantly smitten with Juny.

In his favor Marshall was not compulsively interested in Juny's past. (She suspected he only half believed the stories she told him). But in her mind this was also a point against him. Anymore than she could for him, Marshall couldn't know what the texture of things had been for Juny before they met. She took it for trouble that he put the wrong stresses on the stories she told him about Fortunes Neck.

"It's that we don't *engage*, Marshall," she often complained, though for his part Marshall claimed Juny mumbled and that he missed a lot of what she was saying. She kept him waiting eight years. It took Juny that long to finally understand all the jolliness of romance.

Even in marriage Juny hasn't ever given up a certain removal; sometimes she wishes this was otherwise, other times she doesn't. At those other times Juny thinks detachment is the red ribbon of her temperament. It's the same as if she had moved to France instead of to Boston. If after 20 years in that other country she learned to speak perfect French there would still be moments when a specific way of expressing herself might only be available to her in English. But that's the lot of the émigré. Accept it or don't, it's up to you.

Juny had no reason to come to Fortunes Neck for a long while after Uncle Hodge was gone. He died in 1987, and once she buried him she didn't come back until May, 1992.

It was early on a Saturday morning and she was traveling home from the meeting on consciousness in datasets they hold every year up at Williams College, which had almost been her mother's alma mater. Juny was on the turnpike going east, back home to Boston, when shortly before Canaan she noticed the sign for the Springfield connector. On impulse she turned off and took the highway south to Fortunes Neck.

Twenty years is the shortest period of long-time. After twenty years the past is just far enough away for sentiment to blur perspective, but only a little, so that the grain of the old experience remains available. The landscape of Fortunes Neck was still recognizable. The corn fields were gone, replaced by you-store-it places and a glass office complex; it remained a sort of nowhere, the way it always was.

Driving down Cottage Row was like touring the backlot of a failing movie studio. It wasn't hard for Juny to recognize her street the way it used to be when she was a little girl, but she was more interested in noticing its transformations. There was Mr. Case. It was just eight o'clock in the morning but already he was outside harrowing his flowerbed with a long spade. The last time Juny saw him was when she was back for Hodge's funeral. Mrs. Case had seen her entering Mrs. B's old house and she brought her husband across to carry condolences. That was five years now. Since then Case had cut down the tulip tree where the all-night singing birds used to be. It looked like he was having trouble getting grass to grow in that spot.

Case was never as old as Juny remembered him; at the time he bought the Collins' old house he would have been barely in his thirties. Case had made Juny's former home the cheeriest place on the street, which wasn't hard to do. The house where the Horns used to live, for instance, and Mr.

Potts before them, needed paint and its front lawn was balding. In the house in which Hodge had holed up with Mrs. Bliss three cars were parked on the lawn. Juny had no idea who bought Mrs. B's house or even what they paid for it. In his will Hodge left whatever was realized from its sale to Carmine Mercy; Bob Trammel handled the deal. The cash in her uncle's checking account and $465 they got for selling the car in the garage went to Juny.

As early as her first year of college Juny saw that her decision to stay in Boston at vacations and in summer suited Hodge and Mrs. Bliss. Once they were done with their responsibility to her they wished to be left alone. They weren't mean about it but it was clearly what they wanted. Then Mrs. Bliss died and Hodge never left Fortunes Neck again.

It wasn't only because he didn't drive anymore that Hodge remained where he was. He had no reason to go somewhere else; home is where the heart is. For the nine years that he was alone Hodge walked over Bring Street Bridge each morning to work at the travel agency, and then in the evenings went back home again. His path took him past the stone buttress with which Johnny Collins collided in 1968. To this day it still has a fist-sized piece broken out of it where Johnny skidded into the retaining wall.

After he was on his own Hodge gave up driving entirely, though he never thought of selling his car. On the day he died that car was hibernating in the garage, covered under years of dust, sleeping like a thing underground and waiting for its chance. The young guy who eventually bought it gave the battery a charge and it just started right up. He drove it away. There was still gasoline in the tank.

For years Juny regularly, and then conscientiously, invited Uncle Hodge to come and see her in Boston. Each time Hodge told her plainly, "No." Juny saw him less and less, and then one day in 1988 Lily Meursault phoned Boston to report that Hodge was dead.

Hodge had outlived all of them but Lily, though he had the lightest handhold on life. What does that prove? There is no meaning to be imposed on it. Although it ought to make us suspicious about any connection between outlook and longevity, exactly as the actuarial tables indicate.

Juny drove slowly down the street and was gone before Mr. Case took any notice. She headed back across the bridge and then up Bring Street to Waterhouse Hill.

At the bottom of the hill Juny got out of her car. She pulled her Red Sox cap down over her face and looked around, behaving like a fugitive in the movies. This was to be a quick visit and she didn't wish to meet any of the old neighbors. Later she thought of how improbable it was that any of them could still be around.

With her head lowered she walked up the cracked macadam path to the top of the hill. The place was deserted. At the top she went straight to her mother's marker. The red oak they'd planted there in 1961 was stoutly middle-aged now, and better than 60 feet high. Its gray bark was chunked as if it had been hacked with a knife. At the base of the tree Amy's plaque was half disappeared into the earth, all but invisible unless one knew where to look. Juny probed it with the toe of her rubber shoe. She thought to find a stick and dig out around it, then thought better of that. The further the marker drifted down into the ground the more likely it was to be left in peace. Someday it will be found and exhibited as a proof of history.

In the copse where she and Irene used to play orphan a grocery wagon lay on its side—who would push a wagon to the top of a hill just to tip it over?

Juny turned her face to the west. The air vibrated with the whine of highway traffic from out on the connector. She shut her eyes and lifted up her face to the springtime warmth. It was mid-morning but the bluey moon was still in the sky, staying up late. The moon's vacant face looked down on the Earth, its old home.

The moon reflected light and Juny absorbed it. Light poured through her, down to her shoes. Without turning she knew when Johnny and Amy were with her. She could feel them testing her limbs with their hands, and marveling at how high she'd grown. They fingered the good fabric of her clothing. They stroked her long hair and traced the features of her face. Juny stood up there on the hill for a long while, or until this knowledge passed.

The connector they built turned out not to be such a great thing for Fortunes Neck. Bring Street wasn't a charmed circle after all, but then life is so full of these heavy ironies that half the time no one even mentions it.

The building where Collins P&H used to be had become

a judo academy. But the Bring Street Café was still there, and so was the news dealer and the insurance agent, where for all Juny knew Mr. Parsons still had a desk. The lawyer Bob Trammel had been dead two years and was buried out in Lordshaven. It was in front of Trammel's old office that Juny saw Lily Meursault coming down the street.

Lily was walking with a stringbag full of grapefruits. She would have been about sixty years old then, though she looked hardly older than when she and Johnny used to sit up nights on the sunporch. The last time Juny spoke to Lily was on the Sunday afternoon she telephoned Boston to report that Hodge Weir was dead. Lily even addressed Juny by her correct first name. She must have been reading from a file card.

"That Mrs. Cage you sold your house to," Lily said, "it was her that heard the cat your uncle kept crying for most of a day—meowing, you know? She got interested and went across to see about it. She peeped in—she's that type—and saw Hodge lying on the floor there." Juny listened to Lily's voice for anything suggesting how she felt about the end of the Weirs. Presuming she felt something.

"It's sad," Juny remembered saying on the telephone. "Dying alone." It was an irresistibly conventional thing to say. It didn't tell the half of it, which was just what Juny was thinking even as the words came out of her mouth.

"Doesn't need to be one thing or another," Lily answered, "so long as the whole thing is quick." She meant this as a comfort. "He must have been awfully tired." It was summer but pouring down rain in Boston, dark as December.

"There's a question I want to ask you," Juny said. "About

my mother."

"My, there's a surprise. Yes?"

"Did anyone besides my grandfather know she was pregnant when she died?"

"Who told you?"

"Dr. Bottle let it slip once. Who told *you* is what I'm asking."

"I'm the policeman, remember? It was me who got the job of questioning Bottle. Because I'm a lady, I suppose."

"As a suspect?"

"Bottle wasn't a suspect. There were never suspects. It was your grandfather asked me to go see about him. Your mother had told Doc she thought she might be pregnant, and he made the guess that she'd go and see Bottle."

"Did my father know?"

"Your mother was waiting to be sure before she told him."

"And?"

"And nothing. Doc asked me to keep quiet about it. He thought he was being nice to Johnny."

"My father had the right to know."

"Yeah and I told Johnny pretty quick. Doc never knew I did, unless Johnny told him, which I can't imagine. Any case he was glad to have that information, if you're wondering."

"Why would my grandfather ever suggest hiding it?"

"Dr. Bottle, as you probably don't know, had a reputation in Fortunes Neck."

"He did abortions. Every girl over 15 knew that."

"So anyway Doc argued that if your father knew your mother went to see Bottle he might put the two and two together. His thoughts would get started."

"Why didn't my father tell me?"

"Because he was looking out for you. First you were a baby, and then when he died you were only a little girl. He would have told you. If you'll remember Johnny was very direct."

"Did you think she did?"

"Your mother get an abortion? Who knows? It was your mother's business. And what would knowing do for you?"

"Situate me" Juny wanted to say though what she answered instead was, "Did it make it worse for my father that she was pregnant?"

"Nothing could have made it worse. One thing was real—your mother—and the other was an idea, if you see where I'm going."

"At all he never talked about it?"

"These days I trust my memory of nothing. I may be getting old. But as I recall the only times Johnny ever mentioned it were times he was worried you might be lonely."

"I was hardly ever lonely." Juny felt an intimacy with Lily that day which surprised her. They were like ex-wives of the same man.

"What else didn't I know?"

"Probably a thousand things at least."

At least. Here's one: Why is love the way it is? Juny would nominate that as the open question, well ahead of what happened to her mother. Amy hit her head. She died. But why is love the way it is?

Everywhere are clues.

Months later Bob Trammel sent Juny a small box by parcel post. In it were odds and ends Hodge had entrusted to his lawyer together with a copy of his death certificate, which owing to a spell-check error listed cause of death as "cognitive heart failure". There was also a photocopy of Hodge's will, signed in the large, careful handwriting that always made Juny think of a fourth-grader's penmanship—a thought that made her feel a little mean for having it.

Juny had once in a while wondered—idly and with no sense of grievance—what happened to the money Doc and Jeannine must have accumulated, if from no other source than from the sale of the hose on Ploughman's Road. The answer was in the stack of Hodge's financial statements that Trammel tossed into the box. Between 1984 and the end of 1987 the stocks in which Hodge invested his inheritance melted to nearly nothing; his broker, some guy working from Hartford, liked the big steel stocks too much and about a hundred years too late. The day Hodge died there was about $14,000 left in the brokerage account, which was subsequently liquidated and—Juny presumed—sent to Carmine Mercy. The Weir name and the Weir money both died with Hodge.

In the package Trammel sent was also a severely taped envelope, the Scotch tape on it so old it was brown. **JUNY** was written on it in letters five inches high. Hodge must have worried someone would miss his intent.

The envelope held mementos of Juny's mother. What little there was appeared miscellaneous at first. Juny's birth announcement from *The Springfield Union*. A clip from an unknown paper in 1948 that showed Amy and two other girl scouts raking leaves. "Spring Cleanup on Waterhouse Hill" said the caption.

There were birthday cards Amy sent Hodge. "Congratulations on turning 21—Now you are legally a dolt." There were Christmas greetings from 1955, 1956 and 1957. There was a note that began as a postcard from Fort Sill (a color photograph of Geronimo's grave on the front side) to which Amy stapled two pages torn from a steno pad once she realized there was more to say than she expected.

January 15
Hi from Oklahoma! Hope your trip back to Framingham Christmas night went OK. I was worried about you in all that wet snow. Wow did it come down!

I'm happy to be "home" again—an army wife and boy am I surprised. Good news: They say we can be together most weekends until the baby comes. John has asked for assignment to New York state. Fingers crossed! He has started training in air conditioners and likes it so far.

Thank you for sticking up for me at Christmas dinner. What a weak home that was! I haven't even told John about it, and won't. Don't you either. I wasn't home a day when mother actually suggested—not in so many words but I knew—that I ought to go see Dr. Bottle about my "problem"—the baby! (You know his reputation, right?) Well, that was good for a day of crying and yelling at each other.

Christmas Eve Dad took me for lunch (I don't know how the Bring Street Café stays in business, by the way) (did I already tell you this?) and said if the baby was a girl he would be pleased if I named her <u>Millicent!</u> From what I know of that business no-thank-you. What a *welcome to the world that would be for a brand new baby, who never did anything to anybody. Let the baby tell its own life story.*

Those two really ought to get together!

It now looks like if the baby is a boy we will call him after you know who. If a girl I'm leaning toward "Dorothy" or "June". Right now I like the second best (better?). June is such a pretty name for a woman, and it's the month when the baby will be born. And after April it's my favorite time of the year.

Dad is probably still steamed from the way you stood up for John. Let him! I'm glad you like John, and I know you'll be the greatest uncle ever. You certainly are my favorite brother ever, and I would say that even if I had another one.

Goodbye for now, Hodge—write us sometime why don't you?

Love,

A.

There was a single article out of the *Union* about Amy's disappearance. It carried the photograph Johnny had given Ronald Meursault on the night Amy didn't come home, the one he said made her look like the ethereal type. Under the picture of the pretty girl was the word MISSING. In the margin beside it Hodge had written *our darling*. The indigo in the ink had evanesced with time. The word had been rendered violet.

The Meursaults were no longer in the law-enforcement business. In 1983 Fortunes Neck voted itself out of existence. By then the highway was a more natural boundary than the Mattabesic River. The portion below it—including Cottage Row and the Bring Street business district—more logically belonged to Arcadia. The northern piece of the town above the connector was absorbed by Lordshaven. Lily was finishing her working life as a sheriff on the Pocumtuk County force, deskbound for the most part. She was still living in the house on Nipmuc Street with her seldom-seen mother.

Walking down Bring Street Lily was vivid in a tangerine-colored track suit. She was still eye-catching in her great size, and she was trim and swinging her grapefruits in the sunshine—what *are* the sources of the erotic? The expression on Lily's face was the same as it ever was: alert. Juny knew there'd be no point in stopping to speak with Lily, even if she'd had that impulse, which she didn't. Juny is never sentimental, except once in a while if she thinks about her father. She knew that on Lily the old stories had even less hold. Not the way they'd had on the rest of them.

Goodbye for now.

www.ingramcontent.com/pod-product-compliance
Lightning Source LLC
Chambersburg PA
CBHW031308280626
47169CB00017B/913